DUNCAN'S HONOR

THE AEGIS NETWORK: JACKSONVILLE DIVISION
BOOK SEVEN

JEN TALTY

JUPITER PRESS

PRAISE FOR JEN TALTY

"Deadly Secrets is the best of romance and suspense in one hot read!" *NYT Bestselling Author Jennifer Probst*

"A charming setting and a steamy couple heat up the pages in a suspenseful story I couldn't put down!" *NY Times and USA today Bestselling Author Donna Grant*

"Jen Talty's books will grab your attention and pull you into a world of relatable characters, strong personalities, humor, and believable storylines. You'll laugh, you'll cry, and you'll rush to get the next book she releases!" Natalie Ann USA Today Bestselling Author

"I positively loved *In Two Weeks*, and highly recommend it. The writing is wonderful, the story is fantastic, and the characters will keep you coming back for more. I can't wait to get my hands on future installments of the NYS Troopers series." *Long and Short Reviews*

"*In Two Weeks* hooks the reader from page one. This is a fast paced story where the development of the romance grabs you emotionally and the suspense keeps you sitting on the edge of your chair. Great characters, great writing, and a believable plot that can be a warning to all of us." *Desiree Holt, USA Today Bestseller*

"*Dark Water* delivers an engaging portrait of wounded hearts as the memorable characters take you on a healing journey of love. A mysterious death brings danger and intrigue into the drama, while sultry passions brew into a believable plot that melts the reader's heart. Jen Talty pens an entertaining romance that grips the heart as the colorful and dangerous story unfolds into a chilling ending." *Night Owl Reviews*

"This is not the typical love story, nor is it the typical mystery. The characters are well rounded and interesting." *You Gotta Read Reviews*

"Murder in Paradise Bay is a fast-paced romantic thriller with plenty of twists and turns to keep you guessing until the end. You won't want to miss this one..." *USA Today bestselling author Janice Maynard*

BOOK DESCRIPTION

In a race against time to find her missing sister, two firefighters find themselves bound by love and a secret that could change everything.

Firefighter Duncan Booker gave his heart once, only for it to be charred beyond recognition. Though he still dreams of having it all—the career, the wife, the family—he can't bring himself to take the leap. That changes at his best friend's wedding, where he finds solace in the arms of Chastity Jade, a captivating firefighter and colleague. Duncan has admired Chastity since she first joined the station, but after one passionate night, they agree to remain

just friends—at Duncan's insistence due to his
lingering fears.

Chastity, familiar with heartbreak, decides to focus
solely on her career after their night together.
However, her resolve lasts only a month when she
discovers she's pregnant and her younger sister goes
missing. Desperate for help, she turns to Duncan,
who readily agrees, unaware of the baby. As they
search for her sister, they navigate a maze of
betrayal and lies, uncovering a love so profound it
reignites their hearts.

For Gabby.

NOTE FROM THE AUTHOR

Hello everyone!

It is important to note that this book was originally titled *Burning Desire* and written as part of the Susan Stoker *Special Forces: Operation Alpha* world. Since the rights to the book have reverted back to me, I have stripped the story of all the elements from Susan's world (as it was legally required of me to do so) as well as changing the names of some of my characters so it would fit nicely into my Aegis Network series.

I have also expanded the story, adding scenes and updating a few things. I'm much happier with the storyline and characters now. I've always loved this series, but as with many things that I wrote years ago, I felt as though I could have done better.

Please enjoy!

Jen Talty

WELCOME TO THE AEGIS
NETWORK

The Aegis Network is the brainchild of former Marines, Bain Asher and Decker Griggs. While serving their country, Bain and Decker were injured in a raid in an undisclosed area during an unsanctioned mission. Instead of twiddling their thumbs while on medical leave, they focused their frustration at being sidelined toward their pet project: a sophisticated Quantum Communication Network Satellite. When the devastating news came that neither man would be placed on active duty ever again, they sold their technology to the United States government and landed on a heaping pot of gold and funded their passion.

Saving lives.

The Aegis Network is an elite group of men and women, mostly ex-military, descending from all branches. They may have left the armed forces, but the armed forces didn't leave them. There's no limit to the type of missions they'll take, from kidnapping, protection detail, infiltrating enemy lines, and everything in between; no job is too big or too small when lives are at stake.

As Marines, they vowed no man left behind.

As civilians, they will risk all to ensure the safety of their clients.

"Hey, wait up."

Chastity Jade glanced over her shoulder, trying not to trip in her three-inch heels as she stumbled down the road headed toward home just a few blocks away. Spiked shoes were not her thing. Nor were dresses. It had less to do with being a tomboy her entire life, and more to do with her lack of grace.

Klutzbutt, as her family called her.

Sometimes she really missed the simplicity of her childhood. Even with all the rules and expectations that came with growing up in such a tight religious community, there had been something to be said for the safety and security it had once provided.

Where the big bad world, as her mother described anything beyond their farm, could cause her heart such grief and chaos.

Still, she wouldn't trade the life she'd come to know for what she'd left behind.

"You shouldn't be walking home alone," Duncan Booker, a fellow firefighter, called out as he jogged across the street. His suit coat was draped over his shoulder, his tie pulled loose, and the first two buttons of his shirt were undone.

A warm shiver glazed over her body like soapy shower water. Duncan should be the front cover for the fireman puppy calendar.

And he'd made for a damn sexy groomsman, even though the wedding had been small, only consisting of what Buddy and Kaelie considered family and those they worked with at the fire station and the Aegis Network.

"Because our neighborhood is so dangerous," she said with an eye roll, waiting for him to catch up. She'd tried to get the man's attention for the past six months or so. Every once in a while, she thought she might have succeeded, but tonight, when he brushed her off, she'd finally had to admit defeat.

He just wasn't that into her, and she supposed

she shouldn't be surprised. They both had exes that they constantly talked about, making it hard to draw the line between friendship and flirting. At first, she thought they were bonding over a shared experience. She used it as something to bring them closer together. When that didn't work, she tried not talking about her ex, but all Duncan seemed to be able to chat her up about was exactly that.

Or his stupid-ass ex-girlfriend.

It really was time to wave the white flag, which is exactly what she'd done when she'd slipped out of the party right after he'd refused to even give her one slow dance.

So why the hell was he chasing her down now?

"I've watched you fall three times tonight without having any alcohol, and now that you've had a few drinks? Well, I don't want you getting hurt."

"Yeah, yeah, yeah." She couldn't wait to kick the damn things off, drop the dress, and put on a pair of shorts and a T-shirt. She felt totally out of her element. "I let Rex's wife, Tilly, do my makeup. I look like a damn clown."

"Not even close. You look quite pretty, though you don't need the makeup. You're beautiful no matter what."

"Why, Duncan Booker, are you giving me a compliment? Or are you just drunk?" As long as she'd known the man, he'd waffled between being sweet and flirty and practically ignoring her.

"You dress up real nice." He took his coat and wrapped it over her bare shoulders. The temperature had dropped, but chilly was still at least ten degrees away.

Slipping her hands through the sleeves, she glanced into his russet eyes, and her heel twisted, causing her body to shift as her ankle gave way.

"Shit," she muttered, grabbing his thick biceps before she face-planted on the asphalt.

He laughed. "Hop on." He stepped in front of her, offering her a piggyback ride.

"What are we, twelve?"

"Just do it before you break your leg."

She hiked up her dress and jumped on his back with more gusto than she planned. He stumbled before his fingers curled around her thighs, digging into her bare skin, sending warm pulses to all the places that made her a woman.

His dark hair smelled like coconut, and she wanted to ruffle it. What the hell? It was always too perfect anyway. She dug her nails in and gave the strands a good tug.

"Hey. Not the hair. It takes a lot to get it to look this good."

"You do have great hair." She rested her chin on his shoulder and let out a long breath. Working with him had been easy. He always treated her with respect. He never made her feel as though she didn't fit in because she was a woman. Or because she was younger than most of the guys. Not one time did he ever try to do things for her or expect she couldn't handle something because of her sex. However, outside of work, they could be awkward in each other's presence. For her, it was all the pent-up raw sexual desire that he brought out.

She had no idea what his problem was since he often acted like she had the plague.

The warm Florida air tickled her pores. The white full moon glowed high. The stars filled the sky in abundance. She took in a deep breath and let her eyelids drift shut. "It was a nice wedding."

"Romantic, small, and quiet," he said. "Very fitting for the bride and groom."

"I can't get over how much Buddy's twin sister is like him. It's weird." She opted to divert the conversation from anything having to do with romance, even though she was the one who brought it up.

"Try dating her." He cocked his head, catching her gaze.

A hum filled her throat. If there were ever a perfect specimen of a man, it would be Duncan. He might as well have been a Greek god at five-eleven of solid muscle, tan skin, smoky eyes, and a devilish smile.

Okay. She had most definitely consumed one too many drinks tonight.

"You dated Kelly?" she asked. "And Buddy let you live to tell the tale?"

Duncan laughed. "I took her out a couple of times and while she's a great girl, she's way too much like my best friend, and it just got all mucky."

"Mucky?" She adjusted herself on his back, draping her arms over his shoulders. "That kind of word only comes out of your mouth when you're buzzed."

"Speaking of which, do you have any beer at your place? I'm going to need to quench my thirst after hiking you all the way home. You're heavier than you look."

She slapped the back of his head. "That's just mean."

"I was kidding. Well, not about the beer."

For the next block, they remained silent. She

concentrated on the night sounds of crickets and an owl hooting in the distance instead of the sexy man who carried her down the street. At twenty-six, she had her entire life ahead of her, and it wasn't that she was in a rush, but she wanted it all. Career, kids, the whole ball of wax, and she wanted it sooner rather than later. The one thing she took from being raised a Mennonite was a strong sense of family.

The rest of it, she'd turned her back on when she left home at age eighteen, something she worried her parents might never truly forgive her for. It wasn't just that she chose to leave her roots behind. Being the oldest, it seemed she inspired curiosity in her younger siblings.

"Keys?" Duncan asked, snapping her mind back to the present.

"Here." She pulled them from her clutch, wondering why he didn't just set her down on the stoop. Instead, he carried her into the kitchen, where he set her ass on the counter, then turned, his body snug between her legs. Every muscle tightened with pure delight, but he was just being nice.

Yeah. That had to be it.

Duncan had no interest in her because his heart still belonged to his ex.

And something about being too old. But that

7

was something he'd let slip one night months ago after a few drinks and stroll through the hood.

"Let's get these off your feet before you kill yourself." Gently, he lifted her leg, his fingers sizzling across her ankles as he slipped the black heels from her feet.

She tried not to moan, but her vocal cords defied her wishes. "What are you doing?" she asked as he wrapped his arms around her waist, his hands running over the top of her ass.

She should have asked herself the same question when she purposely placed her hands on his broad shoulders, arching her back. While she felt the alcohol, she wasn't so drunk that she didn't understand the vibe she sent Duncan.

Only, she'd been sending it for months, and he had ignored it all but maybe a half dozen times and one kiss.

Just one. But it knocked her socks off.

"Something I probably shouldn't be doing," he whispered, leaning in, brushing his lips over her mouth.

She closed her eyes and sucked in his tongue, swirling it around with hers, throwing caution to the wind. She hadn't come this far in life without taking risks.

Unfortunately, he pulled away. "We work together, which complicates things and you're so young."

"Me being ten years younger bothers you?"

"Try almost thirteen and it's not that as much as the fact that your ex always shows up in different places, and you don't seem to turn him away." Duncan arched a brow.

She cocked her head. "Seriously? You're going to bring him up while my legs are wrapped around your waist." Before he could back away, she locked her ankles together, pulling him closer.

He groaned.

"You either want me, or you don't," she said, wishing she'd kept her mouth shut because it didn't sound sexy at all. "And don't use my age as an excuse again. I'm not a child."

"Oh, I want you all right. But I don't know if I can give you more than a good time, and I'm not into being with someone else's—"

She covered his mouth. "You watched me toss him out on his ass a few months ago, and that was the last time he showed up. Why are you using that as an excuse to walk out that door?"

Only, she knew the answer, and her name was Robin. Duncan had been head over heels in love and wanted the world with her, but Robin broke his heart into a million pieces.

His thick lashes fluttered over his whiskey-colored eyes. He opened his mouth and shut it at least five times.

"Look, I'm not asking for anything." She hoped her voice hadn't trembled like her insides. "But a good time." What a lie. However, if she couldn't have him forever, one night might get him out of her system.

"Chastity, I should go."

She cupped his face. "Why are you still pining over Robin? What made her so special? Tell me." She bit down on her lower lip. Clumsy and diarrhea of the mouth. Not a good combination. "Why can't you get over her?" She had no right to get up in his face, which certainly wouldn't help her get him in bed. "Forget it. You're right. This was a bad idea." She unclasped her legs, dropping her hands to the countertop. "Thanks for walking me home. I appreciate it."

"For your information, I'm over Robin. That's not the problem here." Holding her gaze, he leaned closer. His hot breath scorched her skin. "You're a good person. Kind. Sweet. Even if something were to happen, it would only be one time. Are you prepared for that?"

"You're the one who chased me down the street."

He traced her lower lip with his thumb. "You'd been dropping hints all night. I was just responding to that."

"Duncan. No offense, but I can't say that I'm looking for a serious relationship. Been there, done that, not ready to rinse, wash, and repeat."

He took her legs and wrapped them around him again as his mouth crash-landed on hers. Their teeth smacked as their tongues twisted and turned over each other. His hands groped at her dress, tugging at the zipper in the back. She wiggled out of his coat and pulled at his tie, desperate to feel his bare skin.

She didn't care about anything other than being in his arms. If this was all she would get, then she'd manage to live with that.

Or at least that is what she told herself.

As he lifted her off the counter, she let the dress the pool at her feet. She stood before him in nothing but a tiny yellow thong. She'd never been ashamed of her body, but in that moment, the urge to cover up forced her hands to cup her breasts. She didn't know why. He stared at her with adoring eyes as he undressed, eagerly tossing his shirt to the table and kicking out of his pants before taking her into his arms.

"You're so pretty," he murmured, circling his fingers around her wrists and tugging her hands from her chest. "You're amazing just as you are."

His hands glided up and down her back while his lips burned tiny kisses on her neck, making his way to her breasts.

She gasped as he took her tight nipple into his mouth. Her breath came in short, choppy pants. She'd fantasized many times about what it would be like to be with Duncan and not even one had her reeling like this. His touch was both gentle and scorching. He made her feel like she was the only woman in the universe for him, which was crazy.

This would be one night. And then she'd have to pretend like it meant nothing.

He looked up at her as he dotted her belly with sweet kisses, his fingers rolling her panties over her hips. "You're special, Chastity, and you deserve better than me."

She hadn't time to ask what the hell he meant by that as he hoisted her back onto the counter and kissed her intimately. His velvet tongue glided over her, and in her in a way, no one else had ever touched her. It was soft yet carried the pressure to take her to new heights.

Threading her fingers through his hair, she pressed her heels into his shoulders. She watched him with awe, enjoying every lap of his tongue and stroke of his fingers.

"Duncan," she whispered, tugging at his head. Her body quivered.

But he didn't take heed. No. He dug in deeper. Harder. Faster.

She couldn't fill her lungs with enough air. They burned with every sharp breath. When she'd first left her community, the idea of having sex before marriage had still been a foreign concept. It hadn't been until she'd turned twenty that she even considered it.

It hadn't gone quite as planned, but at least the young man she'd been with had done his best to make it comfortable. They dated for a few months, but she didn't love him.

But she did love Duncan.

Over the years, she had a few lovers and a few long-term relationships with fantastic sex, but no one made her feel like Duncan right now in this moment. It was as if he worshipped her body like a temple, his only focus on her pleasure.

Her stomach trembled on the verge of release. She tried to hold back, savoring the sensations as every cell erupted like a massive volcano.

"Oh God," she said with a throaty moan, her thighs clamping down over his face as her body jerked. Before she knew what hit her, he'd lifted her from the counter as he sat in one of the kitchen table chairs, lowering her over him. "Oh my God." He slid inside like he was made just for her. Rocking back and forth, she kissed him, tasting herself on his sweet lips. She rolled her hips over him, desperate to please him.

He held on to her hips, pushing her back and forth in the same desperation. Their mouths joined much in the same way as their bodies moved against each other in the heat of raw passion. His hands roamed her skin, molding her muscles as if she were wet clay waiting to be transformed into art.

The orgasm building inside promised to rock her wildly, sending her to a place she'd only dreamed about.

With Duncan.

And now it was happening for real.

She wanted to pinch herself.

He buried his face in her neck, nibbling at her earlobe, whispering her name as he groaned and grunted, and then something akin to a low howl echoed in her ears.

Even her wildest fantasy hadn't come close to what he did to her body, mind, and soul.

"Duncan," she cried out, digging her fingernails into his muscles. Thank God they were cut short, or she might have drawn blood. Her moans filled the air like a foghorn on the river. Loud and proud.

He cupped her ass, holding her still.

Neither one could catch their breath as their chests heaved into each other, clashing like waves smashing on the beach. She rested her head on his broad shoulder, trying to calm her pulse. Her legs squeezed around his waist, and she needed to hold on to him for a bit longer.

For the next five minutes, he showered her cheek and neck with soft kisses while his fingers danced up and down her spine in a loving caress. It was so tender she thought that perhaps he cared a little more than just a man and a woman sharing a night of the purest form of sexual release.

But as loving as he was, he also began to pull away—not physically but emotionally and mentally.

She could tell by the way his body tensed and his touch changed to what felt like an obligation, not a man caving to a woman's desire.

Buddy had warned her that he might push her away if she continued to pursue him. He'd been distant with everyone ever since he and Robin broke up.

Hell, her entire team had warned her that Robin had messed him up so badly that he might never recover.

But no one would tell her why.

What the hell had he just done?

Chastity deserved someone who could give her everything she wanted, and Duncan wasn't that man.

Not now. Perhaps never. No matter how much he cared about her, his heart still ached for what he might have lost. He couldn't explain the pain that had wormed its way into his soul, but it was wedged so deep he couldn't see past it.

And he'd tried.

He wanted to allow himself to move from the past and into the present, but every time he tried, what happened smacked his memory like a speeding bullet. It was a relentless assault and now he'd pulled one of the sweetest women he knew into battle.

Fuck. If he listened closely to himself, he'd realize how much better off he was without Robin and her lies.

Yet he wasn't sure Chastity was what he needed.

Still, he'd made love to her anyway.

If you could call what they did in her kitchen *making love*. No, that was more like desperate fucking by two insanely horny people who didn't think through the ramifications of what would happen next.

He hiked up his pants, staring at her wearing only his dress shirt, leaning against the very counter he'd given her the first orgasm. It was hard to bite back a smile remembering it, but it immediately turned into a frown. He turned, and his mood soured even more as he stared at an image of her dick ex-boyfriend.

Over him? Duncan thought not. Well, at least he didn't have to worry about her getting hung up him. That should make him feel better, but it didn't.

"You're regretting this, aren't you?" she asked.

He had to credit her for sounding confident and strong when asking such a question.

Shifting his gaze, he threaded his fingers through his hair. "No. I don't think I could regret that, but—"

"The word *but* implies regret." She folded her arms over her chest, crossing her ankles.

God, the woman had some serious sex appeal. But what killed him was how intelligent and kind she was—always giving of herself to everyone. He wished he could get his head out of his ass. If he could ever love another woman again, it would be someone like Chastity.

No. It would be Chastity.

Only, she was in love with someone else, a point driven home by that damn picture.

And his heart hardened and twisted just thinking about ever trusting another woman again.

"It's not regret. But you and I aren't a good idea. Working together could be tough, and I hope it won't be awkward for either of us two days from now."

"That's not your problem, and it's just an excuse."

He arched his brow. "And what exactly is my problem, then?"

"You're afraid. I get it, so am I."

"The only thing I'm afraid of is that you're not over him." He pointed to the picture on the counter.

"I'm so over him."

"Then why is the picture still there?" Jesus. Now he sounded like a goddamn jealous boyfriend.

"It's a good one of me and my siblings, and I didn't feel like cutting the asshole out, ruining a perfect picture."

That was a fair enough response. Only, he had a few good ones of him, Robin, and his buddies, and he wasn't displaying them in his house anymore.

"But since we're on the subject, the real reason you don't want to take a chance on me is you're afraid I'll turn out just like Robin. What the hell did she do to you?"

He closed his eyes, taking a deep calming breath. He repeated that five times before blinking. "I'm sorry. You are a special woman and someday your prince will come, but it's not me."

"Now you're just being a dick."

He let out a sarcastic laugh. "Maybe. But I'm being honest. I like you. And if I thought things wouldn't get weird, I'd say let's do it again. But I don't want to hurt you, and in the end, that's what will happen."

"I believe only half of that. The rest is you're afraid I'll hurt you. Well, I'm not Robin and while I have no idea what she did, I highly doubt I'd be the kind of girl to do it. But if you want to go on as if this didn't happen, then I can do that." She shrugged, but he noticed she had a difficult time swallowing.

Yeah, he was an asshole for hurting her like this, but if he didn't do it now, letting it drag on for a couple of dates or a few months, it would make more than his and her life hell.

It would make everyone else at the station house go bonkers and he couldn't have that.

He scratched his chest, feeling the sharp squeezing pain he had every time he thought about the baby Robin had aborted.

Only this time, the cause of the pain had been his inability to get close to Chastity. He'd been thinking about her for months and always enjoyed her company, but no matter how much he wanted her, his heart wouldn't allow anyone in, not even her.

"I'm sorry, Chastity. I really am."

"I know," she said. "Let me go get some clothes on and I'll give you your shirt back."

He stood in the middle of the kitchen as she disappeared into the bedroom. He wouldn't be there when she returned.

Hopefully, they could put this in the past and remain friends.

He slipped from her house into the night, resigned that he'd spend the rest of his life alone.

"I'm not pining for her," he whispered. "I'm pining for the child I thought I'd have."

C hastity pounded Duncan's front door, gripping his white shirt, which she'd washed and ironed. It was the least she could do. Now it was time to go about the business of being friends. Going back to the time before she fucked him in her kitchen.

She refused to call it anything else.

Being crass somehow made her feel better about the whole thing.

The door rattled and Duncan appeared, wearing only a pair of shorts, his hair already perfectly styled for the day. It was rare that it wasn't. Even when he rolled out of his bunk at the station house, it was close to perfection. "Chastity. What are you doing here?"

"Thought it might be less awkward if I returned this now and not at the station." She handed him the shirt on a hanger. "It's clean, pressed, and ready to wear again."

"Thanks. You didn't have to do that."

"Not a big deal."

"I was just making some coffee. Would you like some?" He pulled back the door and waved his hand.

"In the spirit of making things normal again. Sure. I'd love a cup," she said, crossing the threshold. She'd been in his house over a dozen times. The crew often got together after shifts to blow off steam. They rotated houses, though everyone preferred Rex's place. It had a nice pool and all the fancy toys. Or his boat. That was always fun.

But Duncan did have an incredible backyard, for a renter.

And impeccable taste in décor.

"Let me go put a shirt on. I'll meet you in the kitchen."

She looked him up and down with an arched brow. "It's not like you don't strut around the station house like that." She wiggled her finger over his strong pecs.

"I don't strut." He laughed. "And now I feel like

a piece of meat." Resting his hand on her shoulder, he squeezed, before padding off down the hallway, button-down shirt in hand.

She sighed as she made her way toward the back of the house. She lived only a few blocks away, but her place was much smaller. Duncan had three bedrooms. Technically, she had two, but the second one was tiny and she used it for a small office. His kitchen had an island and enough room for a larger table. Hers barely had room for a table for two.

He had two full bathrooms.

She had one.

He had a deck and a large backyard, where she had a small patio and, well, that was it.

But she loved her space. She loved the neighborhood. She had Kaelie and Buddy for neighbors. Duncan too. As well as a few more from the crew. She shouldn't be lonely.

Only, she was.

Removing the mug he'd already made, she found another cup and placed it under the coffee maker. Her pulse ran like a rabbit being chased by a wild animal, but she did her best to remain as cool as a cucumber on the outside.

What was done was done. And she wasn't going

to regret it. Nor did she have plans to repeat it, but she wouldn't be able to put up much of a fight if he wanted to. As a matter of fact, she'd never be able to say no, even if she knew it was for the best.

Duncan would never be hers, something she'd learned last night.

"So, what are you doing this fine Sunday?" Duncan snagged one of the mugs and jumped up on the counter, swinging his legs like a small child. He took a gulp and held her gaze, as if nothing had happened.

Well, fucking good for him.

"My parents would like me to go to church."

Duncan chuckled. "Yeah, I get the same pressure. It's not as persistent. A dig here. A scripture comment there. A reminder about pushing forty and not being married. Sometimes I wonder if my mom is secretly praying I'm a virgin."

Chastity's cheeks flushed at the same time she burst out laughing. "Go through life with my name. It's a constant reminder of the fact that my family's religion dictates the no sex before marriage rule." She crossed her ankles and rested an arm over her middle as she sipped her bitter brew, doing her damnedest not to think about last night.

At least they weren't in *her* kitchen.

But they were in *a* kitchen.

He stared at her for a long, intoxicating moment with his smoldering eyes as if he were reliving every second of their encounter. Right up to the point he regretted it. He cleared his throat. "I was going to call you this morning and apologize for how I left things last night. I didn't handle things well."

"Don't sweat it." She put on her best smile and stuffed down all her emotions. "We'd both been drinking. Not to mention we'd been sending each other mixed messages for months. Now it's out of our systems."

"Are you sure about that?" He eased off the counter and closed the gap. Taking her mug from her fingertips, he set it aside. Using his foot, he uncrossed her legs and pressed himself between her thighs, gripping her hips.

Her chest heaved up and down with every breath she took.

"I didn't think so," he whispered with his lips so close to hers she could taste the hazelnut from his coffee.

It would be so easy to cave to her sexual desires. He clearly wanted her and that stirred something deep in her soul. It ignited an infinite flame. But she needed to take a moment. Needed to regroup. To find her center. To find another way to get him to see her.

All of her.

She pressed her hand in the center of his chest and tilted her head. "You made it clear last night that this couldn't happen again."

"Are you trying to tell me this isn't why you came here?" He cupped her breast, fanning his thumb across her nipple.

Biting down on her lower lip, she arched into his body. "No. It's not. And now you're not playing fair. I'm attracted to you; that's no secret. But I don't want to make this a thing." She dug her nails into his shoulder blades.

"You don't want to make what a thing? Sex with me? Or sex in the kitchen with me?" He had the audacity to wink all while his thumb and index finger pinched and twisted her nipple.

She couldn't think straight while he did that, and something told her he knew that.

"Both," she managed between raspy gasps for air.

"Then why did you honestly come to my home at eight in the morning?"

"To return your shirt because bringing it to the

station would have raised a few eyebrows and forced an explanation. My sex life isn't up for discussion. With anyone."

He nibbled on her earlobe. "That's good to know, because neither is mine." He bent over, grabbing her from behind her knees and lifting her off the floor.

"Whoa. What are you doing?"

"Moving this to the bedroom, so it doesn't become a kitchen thing." He carried her with ease down the hallway.

"Whatever happened to this couldn't happen again?" While she wanted him—and this—in the worst way, she needed to understand him and what he was thinking.

"Are you trying to talk me out of it?" He kicked open the bedroom door and stumbled onto the mattress, propping himself up on his elbows, fanning her cheeks with his thumbs, staring into her eyes with those intense dark orbs of his, driving her mad with desire.

"No, but nothing has changed from last night. You have two misconceptions about me and—"

He pressed his finger over her lips. "I'll concede you could be over that dipshit you were dating.

However, I'm not emotionally available. I can be your friend. We could do this a few times, but it won't be anything meaningful. If that makes me an asshole, then I'll wear that title."

She palmed his face. "Am I slut for wanting this without the strings of a relationship attached to it?"

"Don't ever call yourself that again." He narrowed his stare. "You're better than that and no, there's nothing wrong with wanting something that isn't serious."

"Good. Now can we please stop talking and get naked?" She'd lost her mind. And Duncan was right. In the end, she would be the one hurt. But she was a fighter. She was strong. She'd made this decision.

Last time.

Then back to the business of being friends.

She'd make sure of it.

———————

Duncan ripped off his shirt with more gusto than he would have liked. His heart hammered in the center of his chest. The anticipation of being with Chastity again filled his soul with the kind of hunger he'd never experienced before and utterly terrified him.

And excited him at the same time.

He grappled with her clothing like a horny teenager. He needed to feel her hot, sultry skin pressed against his as they lay in his bed. He tried to slow down, to enjoy the moment, but he couldn't get enough.

Their bodies collided with a fiery passion, igniting a primal desire that consumed Duncan. It reminded him of the first fire he'd ever fought. That had been what he'd been born to do. Whether it be in the Air Force or as a civilian, it was the air that he breathed.

Chastity's fingertips traced the lines of Duncan's chest, sending shivers down his spine. Her lips met his in a searing kiss, their tongues dancing in a tantalizing rhythm. She was the kind of woman he could blissfully lose himself in and never search for the surface again.

He couldn't believe how much he wanted her, how much he needed her in that moment. The room filled with the sound of their ragged breathing and the intoxicating scent of their combined desire.

Last night, he told himself he could have her

once and that would be the end of it—one taste, and he'd be able to walk away.

Then she showed up this morning and he'd talked himself into one more time. This was all about getting her out of his system. If he didn't, how on earth would he ever be able to work with her again?

Duncan's resolve crumbled like sand slipping through his fingers. His hands roamed over Chastity's curves, memorizing every dip and rise of her skin. The passion between them blazed hotter with each tender touch, igniting a hunger that could not be quenched.

Chastity arched against him as Duncan's lips trailed a path of fire down her neck, leaving a trail of goosebumps in their wake. The room seemed to shrink around him, the outside world fading away until there was only the two of them locked in an erotic dance.

In that moment, all thoughts of walking away vanished from Duncan's mind, replaced by a single-minded determination to savor this experience with Chastity.

He'd deal with the consequences later.

Only, he'd make sure he didn't hurt her. No.

He'd do whatever it took to ensure that her feelings were protected.

God, he hoped what she'd said was true and that this was purely physical for her too.

Who was he kidding? He cared for Chastity.

He just couldn't have her. Not that way.

Needing to push her over the edge, he thrust himself deep inside her.

Chastity arched, moaning. She accepted him as if they fit together. "Yes, Duncan. Please," she begged.

Duncan couldn't help but smile as he felt her arms encircle him, the gentleness of her touch contrasting perfectly with the raw passion.

Her climax collided with his like a submarine exploding to the surface. It shocked his system. He hadn't been prepared for it and he held her so tightly he thought he might break her.

She was so warm, so soft, like the embrace of a long-lost love.

He kissed her tenderly, doing his best not to immediately retreat. Because he desperately needed to.

Her eyes held a depth of emotion that spoke volumes. He knew he was playing with fire, but the pull to be with her, to feel her in every way possible, had been too strong to resist.

But as he stared into her eyes, the seriousness of the situation dawned on him—they couldn't do this. He couldn't do this.

He pulled away slightly, reluctantly, and searched her gaze for any indication of regret or resentment. Thankfully, he found none.

"We can't do this again," he said softly, a hint of desperation tinging his voice. "We can't keep doing this."

Chastity nodded. "I know. There are so many reasons it's a bad idea." She smiled. It was genuine. "But know I'll never regret this and I hope you won't either."

"Nope." He kissed her nose. "But we have to find a way to put the genie back in the bottle."

"Well, the genie usually grants three wishes."

"Oh my God. That's not helping." He rolled to his side, pulling the blanket over their bodies. "Especially when you're naked. In my bed."

She raised up on her elbow and patted his chest. "I was kidding."

The sound of a truck pulling into his driveway caught his attention. He glanced at his watch. "Fuck." He jumped up from the bed and tossed a few articles of clothing at Chastity. "You might want to hurry up and get dressed."

"Why?" She sat up, clutching her shirt to her chest, but it did nothing to cover up her perfect breasts.

He blinked. "Um, well, Arthur, Rex, and Kent are here."

"What the hell." She leaped from the bed. Her feet tangled in the comforter, and she face-planted on the floor.

He couldn't help it. He chuckled.

"Not funny," she mumbled.

Bending over, he lifted her to her feet and helped her dress, doing his best not to touch too much, but he did let his gaze soak in every inch. He burned the memory of her body into his brain because he wasn't going to allow himself to see it again.

"Why are they here?" She wiggled into her shorts.

"We've got a meeting at the Aegis Network in an hour." He turned and fiddled with his hair in the mirror. "I kind of forgot. Or should I say someone distracted me."

"You distracted yourself. I was just returning your shirt."

He glanced out the window. "You have about thirty seconds to get to the kitchen and act casual. Not sure what we'll say about why you're here."

"That's easy. You're explaining why half my herbs are dead." She turned and took two steps toward the door.

He grabbed her by the waist. "You've got to be kidding me. You just planted them."

She shrugged.

"We'll actually really talk about that another time." He gave her a little love tap on the ass, which he probably shouldn't have. Now all he needed to do was make the rest of this somewhat normal. The last thing he needed was to have anyone at the station house know he'd slept with Chastity. Not because he was embarrassed or ashamed or regretted it. None of those things were true.

But because the last thing either one of them needed was razzing from the rest of the crew.

Squaring his shoulders, he made his way to the front door and opened it. "You three are about fifteen minutes early."

Arthur glanced between Rex and Kent. "Good morning, Chastity."

Duncan swallowed as he glanced over his shoulder.

"Right back at you." Chastity carried a to-go mug in one hand and a small plastic bag in the other.

"What are you doing here bright and early?" Kent asked with a smug grin.

"Me and my black thumb killed all my herbs that Duncan helped me grow." She held up the little baggie. "I needed some rosemary, so I came over to steal some." She shoved the mug in his chest. "I thought you might like to finish this. Call me when you've got time to help me replant my shit. You boys have a nice day."

"I've got a few minutes. I'll walk you home," Duncan said.

She patted his chest. "Right. Because at nine in the morning, this hood is so dangerous." She waved her hand over her head and disappeared out the door.

Arthur arched a brow. "Did she spend the night?"

"I was about to ask the same thing," Rex said.

"She did not." At least Duncan wasn't lying.

"Damn, I was hoping something was finally going to happen between the two of you." Kent shook his head.

"We're just friends and it's going to remain that

way." Duncan snagged his keys and slipped his feet into his boots.

"Too bad," Arthur said. "That woman would be good for you."

But Duncan couldn't get his head out of his ass and trust that she wouldn't do exactly what she said he was afraid of.

And that was hurt him.

Chastity sat at the table in the kitchen at the station house, staring at her spaghetti and meatballs. The beginning of the shift had been a little crazy. A four-car pileup on the highway, followed by a fire, a lightning strike, a call by an old lady whose husband had fallen out of his wheelchair and she couldn't get him up off the floor, and finally, a man got his dick stuck in a jacuzzi jet.

Now, that one she'd never seen before and she hoped she'd never see it again.

It was an unusually busy and slightly odd morning.

All the men in the station house had been

walking around as though their manhood had gotten stuck somewhere.

"Hey." Duncan shuffled into the kitchen. "Any more of that?" He wiggled his finger over her food.

They hadn't seen each other since the morning they had sex. That was three days ago. He'd texted that he wouldn't be home for a few days because of an assignment with the Aegis Network. That was nice of him but wasn't necessary. Although, he'd been doing weird shit like that for months.

Random texts.

Random phone calls asking her if she wanted to have a drink. Or go for coffee. Or just hang out. Nothing would ever happen. But there would be awkward silences. Long gazes. His hand on the small of her back.

Today, they'd barely said two words before their first call had come fifteen minutes after their morning meeting, not giving them a chance to be awkward.

Since then, they'd been too busy.

Thank God for small favors.

"There's tons left." She waved her fork. "And while you're in there, you can grab me another slice of that garlic cheese bread. Or two."

He laughed. "No idea how you stay so tiny eating all those carbs." He rested his hand on the back of her neck and gave it a good massage.

"By running every morning with you." Unable to resist, she dropped her head and moaned. "God, that feels good."

"It's been a long day." His fingers snaked across her shoulders, hitting all the right muscles. This right here was why half the station house busted both of their balls about a storm brewing.

"Where is everyone? It's too quiet in here." She stiffened her spine. This wasn't appropriate for two people trying to forget they'd ever slept together.

"Arthur is in his office with Rex. The rest of the crew is napping or watching something in their bunks, hoping it's a quiet night." He shifted. "And that we don't see weird shit, because I never want to see a man with his—"

"Don't say it. Just the thought actually makes my girly parts hurt."

"Imagine what it does to my manly parts." Duncan visibly shivered. "It would be nice to have a few hours of absolutely nothing. I'm exhausted." Duncan made his way to the fridge where he took out the pasta that Garrett had made before the last call. He dumped a large portion on a plate, shoving it in the microwave. After that, he took out some bread and placed it on another plate. The way he moved about the kitchen only served as a reminder of what had transpired between them.

Her cheeks heated.

Quickly, she stuffed her mouth full of pasta.

The microwave dinged, and he set his plate next to hers while he warmed the bread.

She'd finish her food and go close her eyes for a little bit. But she wasn't going to run from Duncan. She needed to show him—and herself—that things weren't any different than they were before.

Or maybe they were better.

Because he wasn't avoiding her anymore.

He pulled out the chair and scooted in a little too close for comfort. "What did you do on our extended few days off?"

"Unlike you and the rest of this crew, I know how to relax." She laughed. "I read a book. I went to the beach. I binge-watched a show and I Face-Timed with my baby sister."

"Lilly or Serenity?"

"Lilly. The other one, for whatever reason, is mad at me."

"Probably because you're acting like a grown-up and not her partner in crime." Duncan pressed his leg against Chastity's. "She's at that weird age where she's technically an adult, but not really equipped yet to handle all the things that go with it."

"I remember those days well." Chastity broke off some bread and plopped it in her mouth. "I dealt with it by running off, setting a precedent for rebellion. But the difference between Serenity and me, or even Manly and my sister, is that my brother and I had a plan. Manly had my parents' blessing, I didn't. I'm not sure they will ever accept me for who I am, or even forgive me for what I did. But Serenity takes it all to a new level."

"I'm not sure I've ever met a teenager who hasn't done some kiss-off to their parents. I know I did my share of things that crossed the line." Duncan wiped his fingers and mouth on his napkin. "I'm pushing forty, and there are moments when my folks still accuse me of being in that rebellion stage." He twirled some pasta on his fork.

"I find that hard to believe. Your parents are amazing."

"They are pretty freaking awesome." Duncan nodded. "However, there are two areas they struggle with when it comes to my life and I know you can relate."

"They feel like you turned your back on God."

"Which I haven't. I just don't think I need to go to church or believe in the same strict principles as they do, or your parents. I know how that's put a damper on your relationships with your family."

Her chest tightened. Not because of how distant she felt from her family, though that did always cause her some pain. But while she desperately needed her and Duncan to be friends again, it didn't change that her feelings for him hadn't miraculously gone away. "My family still doesn't understand."

"They will. Give them time."

She cocked her head. "What's the other struggle with your parents?"

"Family." He shrugged.

"And you no longer want one," she said as a matter of fact. "Can I ask why?"

"Oh boy. That's a loaded question." He chuckled. "I used to and when I was your age, it's all I could think about. But being in the Air Force made it difficult. Most of the women I dated struggled with my deployments."

"What about Robin?" Inwardly, she cringed. No

one at the station brought that woman up. It had been a little over a year since Duncan and Robin had called it quits and Chastity hadn't been around to see how madly in love they had been.

Or to watch her destroy one of the most wonderful men Chastity had ever met.

"I'd been out of the Air Force for a while when I met her," he said.

"That's not what I'm talking about and you know it."

"She's not worth either of our oxygen and I have something else I'd like to discuss with you," he said. "I'm glad for this moment alone. I wanted to make sure we're okay. That you're okay. We haven't had the chance to talk since that morning."

She arched a brow. "Do I look like there's something wrong?"

"Well, no." He scowled. "I just don't want you to think I go around sleeping with just anyone. Even though I'm not ready for a relationship, with anyone, I'm not a man who uses women. I don't go to bed with someone unless I care about them," he said softly.

"We've covered this. I appreciate that you're concerned about my feelings. I really do. Not to toss this back in your face, but you've mentioned my age and religion a few times. I am twenty-six. I won't deny the fact that's young. Or the fact that my religion taught me that I was supposed to get married and have kids long before I reached this milestone. As a woman, that was my purpose."

"You know what my opinion about all that is."

She smiled and nodded. They had a fair amount in common and she valued how he could straddle both worlds much easier than she could. Her sex made it difficult. Where she came from, men didn't take her seriously. Hell, neither did the women.

Even out here, she had to fight for equality.

Duncan understood that and he always treated her as if she were just another one of the guys.

Until he didn't.

But he managed to do it gracefully and in a way that didn't make her feel as though all he saw were her tits.

"I sure do, and to be fair, at one point, I thought that was what I wanted," she said.

"Let's be honest about that." He rested his arm over the back of her chair. His fingers twisted around her ponytail in an exotic dance that didn't belong at work. "Because I know you and you still want all that one day."

"I do." She nodded. "But not today. And not anytime soon. Right now, I want to enjoy living in the moment."

"I get that. Trust me. I do. However, you're acting as though you're giving up on all those hopes and dreams and I don't understand what's changed. Was it that asshole ex of yours? Or have I done something?" His thumb brushed gingerly across her neck, right under her ear. "Because I don't want to be the person you chase after when I can't offer you anything."

"You're giving yourself too much credit," she said. "Honestly, I'm taking time for myself and enjoying life. Can we leave it at that?"

"Yeah. Of course." He leaned in and pressed his lips against her cheek. "Want to go watch that show we started last week?"

"Sure."

"I'll clean up in here. We can watch in the small room."

"Sounds like a plan." She stood at exactly the same time as he, bumping into his chest.

He gripped her hips and stared into her eyes. "Another time. Another place," he whispered.

"Duncan. Now you're giving me mixed messages. And at work of all places. Don't."

"I'm sorry. I don't mean to be the one having a hard time with what happened and to be honest, as much as I wouldn't mind it happening again, it can't. We both know that." He kissed her palm. "I'll make some popcorn." He gave her a good shove.

Damn, that man was giving her whiplash.

But this was what he wanted and she would have to agree to it. She didn't need a man who had one foot out the door.

And the other one grounded in a relationship with another woman that had ended badly.

She snagged one of the blankets and stretched out on the big sofa. The more she did things with him as they used to, the faster things would go back to the way they were.

Or at least she hoped they would.

But everything felt different. Even the playful banter, which they had always done ever since they had met. The sexual tension had always been there, that neither one could deny.

"Are you going to hog the entire sofa?" Duncan grabbed her big toe before setting a bowl of buttered popcorn on the table. He lifted her feet, swung them to the side, and shifted her body.

She was about to protest, but he lifted the bowl of popcorn, rested it on his knee, and then had the audacity to wrap his free arm around her shoulders, tugging her to his chest. "What the hell are you doing?"

"Watching a show with you, like we've done a million times." He arched a brow. "And if you all of a sudden curl up over there on the other side of the couch like I'm a leper, that will get people talking. Or do I need to remind you of all the times you've fallen asleep with your head in my lap?"

"Which got both of us a fair amount of razzing."

He chuckled. "As did you being at my house the other morning. Or me chasing you down the street after Buddy's wedding. But no one believes I'll ever act on whatever they think they see."

She jerked her head. "Now I'm insulted. That makes it sound like I'm not good enough."

He cupped the back of her neck, drawing her closer. "No. You're too good for me. Hell, you're too good for most men. But that's not even the point." He glanced over his shoulder before kissing her and it wasn't the kind of kiss that was shared between co-workers. His tongue slipped between her lips, twirling around hers in a passionate tango. "Shit," he mumbled, setting aside the popcorn. "I'm going to hit the weight room." He stood and strolled out of the small room.

"Damn it," she whispered. That didn't go as she intended. She touched her lips. What she felt for Duncan was real. It was powerful. And she knew without a doubt, he felt something more than a sexual attraction for her, but whatever this chick Robin had done to him, it had successfully destroyed his ability to open his heart to anyone.

Ever.

Duncan leaned against the sink and stared into his glass of water. He'd tried working out. Then a cold shower. He'd tossed and turned in his bunk for an hour, but he couldn't push Chastity out of his thoughts.

For the sake of their working relationship and friendship, he had to.

Fucking Robin and her damn lies and betrayal. Every time he thought he could get past what Robin had done and move forward, it reached up from the depths of his soul and consumed his heart.

"Wow. You look ridiculously serious." Rex

maneuvered into the kitchen. "No. More like constipated."

"More like traumatized from our last call."

"What man wouldn't be." Rex shook his head. "What grown-ass man sticks his dick there? I mean really, he was forty-six. And not bad-looking. I don't get it."

Duncan chugged his water. "I thought sticking it in a toaster was weird."

"Time to change the subject." Rex jumped up on the counter. "What's really got you out of bed at four in the morning? Because as strange as that call was, that's not what has your wheels turning."

"Just couldn't sleep."

"Bullshit," Rex said. "And I bet she's got a name." He cocked his head. "What the hell is going on with you two?"

"Absolutely nothing."

"Come on, man. We've been friends a long time. Something shifted since Buddy's wedding and it's got you more tense than usual."

Duncan set his glass next to the sink. He wasn't going to discuss what happened with anyone. He wouldn't do that to Chastity. She deserved better than to have what happened between them reduced to watercooler chat. But

Rex was right. Duncan was a ball of nerves. He struggled to compartmentalize his emotions. If he was being honest with himself, that had been a problem before he slept with Chastity. Now that he had, part of him wanted more. But his heart refused him. "You all have been telling me for a while now that I have feelings for Chastity. That I need to put Robin in my rearview and get on with my life. But it's not that simple. And to be honest, I tried."

Rex arched a brow. "What does that mean?"

"It means I talked to Chastity and we're at a weird place because being friends is more important. It's what I want because I can't give her what she needs for the long haul." Duncan sighed. "But now, to be honest, I find myself tempting fate."

"We all know how much you care about her and what I personally don't understand is why you don't go for it."

"There are a million reasons. The two biggest ones are I will hurt her and what it will do to everyone we both work with. It's already started just by me chasing her down after Buddy and Kaelie's wedding. Telling her I was attracted to her, knowing she had feelings for me was a mistake and I can't put that back in the bottle. All I can do now is try to make things normal again. It will take time, but we'll get there."

"From where I'm sitting, it sure as shit doesn't sound like that's what you want." Rex held up his hand. "I don't begin to understand everything that went down between you and Robin. But I do know you're holding on to some major pain there. You've got to let it go. It's not you who's going to hurt Chastity if you get involved with her, but your past and your inability to release it. Trust me on this. I know a lot about that subject and it's slowly killing you just like it did to me."

No one knew about Rex's past with his wife Tilly until she strolled down that dock, unpacking a shit ton of baggage at that man's feet. However, it had turned out to be the best damn thing that had ever happened to Rex.

This wasn't the case for Duncan. Or for Chastity. This situation was very different. "Chastity is young. A better man than me will roll into her life and sweep that girl off her feet and give her everything I can't. It's best if I put a plug on it now and save everyone a little heartache later."

Rex pushed from the counter, letting his feet hit the floor with a thud. "You can tell yourself that lie all you want. But it's going to be your heart that suffers the consequences when you have to sit back and watch her with some other guy. By that time, it might be too late and you'll wish you had gotten your head out of your ass." He slapped Duncan on the shoulder. "If I were you, I wouldn't let that happen."

"I have to."

"Then you're making the biggest mistake of your life." Rex turned and strolled out of the kitchen, leaving Duncan alone with his thoughts.

He pinched the bridge of his nose. He couldn't deny—not even to himself—that he cared a great deal for Chastity. It went way beyond the physical. They shared so many common bonds. At first, he used the age difference to keep her at bay. But that soon disappeared. It was just a number and she was so damn easy to talk to. He related to her in ways he couldn't with anyone else, and that alone was refreshing.

The sound of feet shuffling against the tile caught his attention. He lifted his gaze and his breath got stuck in his throat. "Can't sleep?"

"I got a couple hours in." Chastity managed to make a pair of sweats and a T-shirt look sexy. She snagged a mug and placed it under the coffee machine. She reached for a pod and opened the top before pressing the button. "It's weird being here without Buddy, but Hampton's not a bad guy."

"Nope. He's not. And Arthur got him a job with the Aegis Network."

"I don't know how all you manage to do work for that outfit and do this job. I struggle to keep my head above water, working part-time in the investigator's office with Kaelie." Chastity leaned against the far counter and crossed her arms.

This was good. It was kind of normal and he was damned if he wouldn't keep it that way. Maybe if he didn't bring up that stupid kiss or what happened, things would stay that way. "How is that going? Are you going to get your investigator license? You'd be good at it."

"Thanks, but I don't know. I like the admin part of the job and right now, that's where Kaelie needs me the most. She's got enough investigators in the field."

"That's true, but one more can't hurt, especially when we're always running off with the Aegis Network, something she's constantly complaining about."

Chastity smiled. God, he loved her face and everything about her. "But not once has it ever interfered with this job. None of you have ever let that happen. Besides, Arthur keeps telling me I'm good at managing people and he and Rex want me here doing other shit too."

"You do like barking orders at all of us."

"That I do." She lifted her mug from under the coffee maker. "Are we going to talk about what happened earlier?"

"Nope. We're going to push forward with being friends. It's what we're good at. It's what we need to be. It's what's best for both of us. More importantly, it's what I want."

"All right." She nodded. "But then I need something from you."

"What's that?"

"No more banter. No more neck massages. No more random touching. No more mixed messages. And certainly no more kissing." She blew into the steaming liquid and took a small sip. "I will do my part. What happened wasn't anything so earth-shattering that it can't be put in the past. You're one of my dearest friends and I don't want that to change. But in order for us to get to the other side of this, you have to promise me that there won't be any more crossed signals. It's not fair."

"I agree."

She pushed from the counter. "I'm going to take my coffee and go shower. I'll see you for breakfast."

He stared at her ass as it swayed out of the kitchen. All he could think about was her naked while soapy water lathered her bare skin.

Fuck.

But he'd just made a promise to himself, and to her, and he was going to keep it if it was the last thing he did.

4

Duncan swigged his beer and stared at Chastity while she chatted with Maren, Tilly, Dixie, and Kaelie. It had been a little over a week since he and Chastity had come to their agreement and he'd been nothing short of miserable. He did his best to hide his emotions from everyone. He joked and laughed and tried to act like himself, but it had become impossible.

Chastity had gotten under his skin, and he didn't know how to rid himself of these emotions.

The only problem was nothing had changed because every time he thought about acting on them, fucking Robin and what she had done popped into his brain like a damn nightmare. Intellectually, he knew Chastity wasn't Robin, and

Chastity had a different moral compass. She wouldn't do what Robin had, even under the worst of circumstances. At least not in the same way.

But Duncan still couldn't get it out of his brain.

"Hey, man." Buddy eased into the chair beside him and clanked his beer against Duncan's. "You've been awfully quiet today."

"Just tired," Duncan said. "I worked a detail yesterday for the Aegis Network right after a shift. It wasn't a tough detail. But I haven't slept much in three days and I'm looking forward to crashing after this little party is over."

"Are you sure that's all this is?"

Duncan let out a short laugh before chugging his beer. "If one more person brings up what they think is going on, I'm going to haul off and punch them right between the eyes."

"I get it." Buddy nodded. "But it's me. Not everyone else. I know the whole sordid tale and will call it like I see it. You're holding on to what Robin did simply because you're afraid to feel something real again." Buddy pointed to where Chastity sat with the other ladies in Arthur's backyard. "And that woman makes you feel things that scare the crap out of you."

"I'm not having this fucking conversation again. Not with you. Not with anyone."

Buddy sighed. "Have it your way." He stood. "But she's not going wait around forever for you to get your head out of your ass." He stuck his free hand in his pocket and made his way toward where Rex and Kent stood.

Chastity rose, holding her glass of wine, and padded in his direction. She plopped down in the chair and let out a groan. "So, is everyone giving you the business? Or is it just me?"

He burst out laughing.

"I don't find it funny."

"I don't either. It's just the way you said it and your timing."

"At least we can laugh at it now."

"I'll cheers to that." He clanked his beer against her glass. "What are people saying to you?"

"They want to know if I put you in a foul mood." She held his stare. "I honestly don't know how to respond to that. For the last ten days we've kept each other at a safe distance when we're not at the station. At gatherings, we tend not to hang out and people have noticed. We don't run together anymore, which I honestly miss. Something has to give and I guess it starts right now."

He chuckled. He'd always enjoyed this side of Chastity. Being confident had been a struggle for her and he understood why. He respected it. He only wished that she could be this way all the time. "I've got another assignment with the Aegis Network. It will take me away for a few days, but when I return, we can start running together again. Things can go back to the way they were before." He nearly choked on the last word. He was no longer sure he could do that. Or that he even wanted to.

But this wasn't the time or place to change the narrative he'd been spinning. He needed some space to think and he couldn't do that while she was so close. Being on a mission would give him that distance to sort through his thoughts. To deal with the things that prevented him from moving forward with his life.

To rid his heart and soul of the darkness Robin had left him with and maybe then he could allow Chastity in before it was too late.

"I'd really like that," Chastity said. "I've missed my friend. My confidant."

"I've missed you too." He reached for her hand but jerked it away.

No more random touching.

He needed to respect that.

For now.

Once he had his head clear, he'd form a plan. But he couldn't do that while still grappling with the earthquake that had left him heartbroken. Chastity deserved better and if he were to give this any chance, he owed it to her to be a whole man.

"When do you leave for your assignment?"

"Tomorrow afternoon. I'll be gone for three or four days. Could be shorter. I'll text you updates."

"Just like old times." She smiled.

"No. New times." With more resolve than he'd had in a long time, he vowed to himself he'd be a new man when he returned.

5

Chastity stared at the stick she just peed on with the big, fat, fucking plus sign in the little window.

Pregnant.

She and Duncan had never discussed that possibility.

Nope. The only thing discussed had been that it could never happen again and that her friendship meant the world to him, which she knew without a doubt was true. He'd done everything to make sure they got back on track.

And so had she.

They had been texting nonstop for the last few days while he'd been on assignment with the Aegis

Network. He'd returned yesterday and was planning some party at his place later.

She wrapped the stick in toilet paper and dumped it in the trash. What the hell was she going to do? In a couple of months, she'd have to tell Arthur she was pregnant, which meant everyone would know, and she'd have to tell Duncan way before that.

Fuck.

Stepping from her bathroom, she avoided the kitchen and went straight to the family room. She stood in front of the liquor cabinet, itching for a shot of Jack, but that would be stupid. While she knew she could have an abortion, it went against every belief system she had.

Besides, she wanted children.

She just didn't want to do it on her own.

Nor did she want any man to feel trapped, and that is exactly what Duncan would feel. While she was no closer to understanding what happened between him and his ex, she knew that Duncan could never give his heart again.

He'd made that perfectly clear.

But he was also an honorable man. He would want to do the right thing, and the most significant thing they had in common besides their work was their religious upbringing. A strict Christian family had raised him. He wasn't overtly religious, like his family, but he did still believe.

As did she.

Only neither of them had the same bond to their families' churches. It was if it had been rammed so far down their throats that it had been impossible to resist rebellion.

Her phone buzzed.

Great. Her mother. Just the person she wanted to speak with. Not.

"Hey, Mom, how are you?"

"Have you heard from your sister?" her mother asked with a tightness in her voice that she hadn't had in a long time.

"Which sister?" She had two younger sisters and two younger brothers, though she suspected her mother was talking about Serenity, who was about to turn eighteen, and not Lilly, who was eleven.

"Chastity Elenore, please don't get fresh with me."

She shivered. There was nothing worse than being a grown-ass adult and having your mother call you by your full name. "I'm sorry, Ma, but I haven't heard from Serenity since she called all upset over the last fight you got in, and if you recall,

I phoned you right away. I've been worried about the way she's acting too."

"Really? You ran out of here in the middle of the night the day after graduating high school. And your brother Manly did the same thing."

"Mom. Manly went to college. With your blessing. He didn't do what I did, and I thought we were past all this."

Her mother let out an audible sob. "Serenity is gone."

Chastity bolted upright. "What do you mean, gone?" The last time she'd spoken to Serenity, she'd been dating a boy who not only wasn't on the approved dating list but was actually no good. Chastity had always tried to be there for her siblings, even when she'd left the community, to guide them, help them navigate the outside world, and make good choices.

Manly had also broken from the practice of being a Mannite, but he lived quietly, married a good Christian girl, and avoided trouble.

Serenity, on the other hand, well, she made Chastity look like a saint.

"She didn't come home two nights ago and—"

"She's been gone for two days, and you're just now calling me?" More importantly, why hadn't

Serenity called? For the last few months, Serenity had been bugging her every week about how to leave as soon as she graduated high school. Chastity tried to tell Serenity she needed a plan and that it would be better to get Mom and Dad behind it than to take off like she had.

Crap. She knew why her sister hadn't called. She'd told her little sister to get her head out of her ass and grow up. That it was one thing to want to leave the church, but it was something entirely different to act out.

"Did you call the police?" Chastity asked.

"They're treating it as a runaway teen."

Well, it wasn't the first time Serenity had run away.

"Is she still seeing that boy?" Chastity asked, scratching her head. "What's his name? Joey?"

"We forbade her to see him ever again," her mother said with a gasp.

"Shit," Chastity mumbled.

Her mother broke out in prayer.

It might make her feel better, but it wouldn't change the reality that Serenity had likely run off with this young man.

"Mom, I've got some friends who have contacts with people who know how to find missing teens. Let me contact them, and I'll call you back."

A few sniffles echoed through the phone. "Thank you," her mother said humbly. "Your father and I tried to talk to her about college. We're open to the new world's ways, to a certain point. We are proud of you. You know that, right?"

She sucked in a deep breath and closed her eyes. She wasn't sure her mother had ever said those words, but she'd honestly felt them the day her parents had come to visit her for the first time three years ago. "Yeah, I know."

"I only want what is best for my children."

"I'll be in touch. And Ma?"

"Yes, dear?"

"If Serenity calls or comes home, don't lecture or toss Bible verses at her. Just hug her. Tell her you love her and wait a day before having a serious conversation."

Her mother let out a dry laugh. "Someday, you'll make a great mom."

If her mother only knew she was with child, out of wedlock, she might not utter those words.

Chastity clicked off the phone and stared out the window. The entire team had seventy-two hours off, which meant Arthur, Rex, and Kent were all spending time with their families. Buddy and Kaelie were doing baby things, getting ready for the birth of their twins. The rest of the crew, those that were single, were gathering tonight at Duncan's.

She couldn't wait that long.

Slipping on her flip-flops, she exited the front door and down the path toward Duncan's house. The sun shone bright in the Florida sky. A warm breeze ruffled the treetops. Knowing him, he'd be out in his garden tending to his plants, herbs, vegetables, and berries. God, that man loved black-berries.

He also made the best blackberry cheesecake known to man.

As soon as she stepped onto his property, she could hear the country music playing in the back-yard. Had she not taken that damn test, she wouldn't be so hesitant.

She pushed open the gate and followed the sound of the music.

Bent over a couple of bushes, wearing only loose-fitting jeans, Duncan flexed his muscles as he pushed dirt around. Perspiration beaded down his tanned skin. She could stand there forever and watch him work effortlessly. He was all man, but he had such a sweet and tender side that it was impossible for her not to have fallen in love with him over the last year.

But it wasn't meant to be. Something she had accepted.

He glanced over his shoulder. "Hey, you," he said with a smile, brushing the sweat from his forehead.

"Hey, yourself." She took a moment to look him over from head to toe. His dark hair always looked like he should be a model in some hairstyling book. Chunks of his hair went in different directions, but all by design.

"Shall I turn around and give you a better look?" He smiled and winked. So much for the banter ending.

"I just want your hair," she mused.

"I'll never give away my secret." He took a few steps closer. His gaze scanned her body.

They hadn't done this dance in a while and it shook her to her core. Her attraction to him was as strong as ever, but he'd decided friends was all he was capable of and she needed to respect that.

"What brings you by?" he asked. "Dinner's not till six."

"I need Darius' contact information," she blurted out, seeing no need to beat around the bush. Darius Ford was a buddy of her captain, Arthur Knight, and also a close friend to Gunner, the man who helped Harper bring closure to her sister's murder. Both had been at Kaelie and Buddy's wedding, and both were good men.

Darius' specialty was finding people; right now, she didn't know where else to turn.

"Why? If you don't mind me asking."

"My mom called, and Serenity might have run away."

"Might have?" He took a beer from the cooler on the deck and waved it in her direction.

"Water, please." It wouldn't be long before people asked why she wasn't drinking.

Duncan tossed her a bottle. "Your sister has been majorly rebelling for a while now." Over the last year, long before their one night of wild, crazy sex, she and Duncan would discuss their religious upbringing and their families. He'd always been a good listener, never judging, and understood her plight for freedom without the burden of guilt.

"She's been gone for two days, and last I spoke with her, she'd still been dating that little prick."

"The one you thought was bad news?" He waved to a chair on the deck before settling into the one next to it.

God, she wanted a beer right about now. "I know she's been drinking and that boy smokes pot. My parents tried to lock her away so she couldn't see him, but that obviously didn't work."

"I take it this kid's not a Mennonite?"

"I really don't know. My parents have been trying hard to keep an open mind since Manly got married, and I turned out not so horrible, but ever since Serenity met this guy, she's been ten times worse than before, and I don't blame them for being upset."

"You have the name of this young man?"

"Joey Richards. But that's all I know."

"All right. Well, let me shower while you call Darius." Duncan tossed her his phone. "I'll call Timothy White over at the Aegis Network. I'm sure he won't mind me borrowing a plane to go to Ohio to help find your sister."

Her mouth fell open. "I wasn't asking—"

"I know. But I'm offering. We've got a few days off, and I will have no assignments with the Aegis Network anytime soon. Might as well make good use of the resources in front of us." He chugged his brew before standing.

"What about the party tonight? You're hosting."

"It wasn't really a party. Besides, a lot of people

had made other plans, so it was going to be small. Really small. Passcode on my phone is 242784." With that, he disappeared into the house.

One thing she knew about Duncan was that he always did what he said he would do.

And maybe over the next couple of days, she'd gain the courage to tell him she was going to have his baby.

6

Duncan had been taking cold showers for the last year.

Freezing showers since he'd gotten a taste of Chastity.

For the last few days, it was all he could to contain his growing excitement to tell her that he'd changed his mind.

And now he sat in a four-seat, 850 horsepower Lancair Evolution aircraft, flying the woman who'd been under his skin for months to the small town of Millersburg, Ohio, to her family farm knowing he'd have to set aside his feelings for a few more days.

Not the right time or place.

He'd do anything for any team member,

including lay down his life. So, helping Chastity was an easy choice.

Being around her proved more difficult. So much so, he often contemplated putting in for special missions with the Aegis Network, but every time he went to make the request, he backed out, waiting for his rotation.

But deep down, he knew Chastity had played a large part in that decision, and that had terrified him.

After he'd made love to her, twice, the memory of the overwhelming crushing pain that his ex had caused him gripped his mind and soul so tightly he had to back away. He'd been a coward. He didn't want to be that man anymore.

He wanted Chasity.

"How long until we land?" Her voice crackled through in his ears. His lips tugged into a short smile.

"About forty minutes." He glanced at his copi-lot. Her long blond hair, which she pulled tight in a ponytail at the nape of her neck, cascaded over her right shoulder. Her soft, tanned skin reflected the sun's rays, making her sparkle like a diamond. And her cobalt eyes shimmered with a certain sweetness you could only find in a genuine person. Everything about her tugged at his heartstrings.

"You want to take over the controls for landing?" She had a hundred hours in flight school and could easily pass her pilot test, but she kept putting it off.

"Nope," she said firmly.

"Come on. You've done it perfectly before."

"I know I have, but I prefer to be a passenger, you know that."

"What if I want a break?" He dipped the nose of the plane lower, heading toward a small landing strip not far from her family's farm. He almost felt as if he knew her family after many late-night conversations. Their upbringings were so different, yet so similar. She should have been perfect for him, but she'd left her ex because he was pushing too hard to get married.

And she didn't want to. Or at least that's what he believed.

And Duncan had no longer wanted that life.

Yeah, right.

He'd wanted it in the worst way, but Robin had stolen it from him and he couldn't allow his heart to take it back.

But everything had changed. He just needed the right time to tell Chastity that. And maybe a little courage.

"Come on, Chastity. Land the plane, and then you should sign up to take your test when we get home."

"Why do you push me so hard to get my pilot's license?"

"Because you're good," he said, staring into her soft, ocean-colored eyes. If they were pools, he'd jump in and float around, never to leave. She had to be the smartest person he'd ever met. Bravest too. Not to mention strong. Hell, she was fucking perfect, and he was the moron who was too chicken to tell her how he really felt. "And if you didn't intend to get your license, why do the training?"

"Truth?" Her thick lashes fluttered as she lowered her gaze. Her cheeks flushed.

"Always," he said.

"To spend time with you."

"Huh?" He did a double-take. His heartbeat increased. He'd always known that she liked him more than a friend. It wasn't as if he hadn't returned the feelings, but they spent so much time together as a team, it surprised him she'd take flying lessons to be with him.

"When I first moved here, you commented you wouldn't fly with me without taking lessons first, so I signed up."

He shook his head. "I would have taken you up regardless."

"I wanted to impress you with my skills."

"You impressed me the second you walked into the station house." He'd been enamored by her since their first training session together. So much so that he screwed up and nearly broke his ankle, tripping over the hose. Her instincts as a firefighter were sharper than those of many seasoned firemen. He trusted her with his life.

But he hadn't been able to trust her with his heart.

That was all going to change.

A long silence filled the cockpit. He concentrated on his checklist for landing. A rental car would be waiting for them at the airport, and he planned on going to her parents' first so they could look through her sister's things for clues.

Then, based on what Darius had found out, they would go to the young man's house to ask probing questions. He couldn't wait to land so he could check his email for that information. What little they had didn't seem to add up to anything but trouble.

He glanced at the beautiful woman next to him, who peered out the window, chewing on her fingernail.

"Are you okay?"

She turned her head. "Not really. Going home under these conditions isn't going to be fun."

"Well, you've got me to hold your hand."

"Ah," she said, turning her gaze back out the window. "My one-night stand is my knight in shining armor."

"Ouch. That hurt."

"Sorry. I shouldn't have said that. I'm just stressed."

"I understand." If he weren't preparing to land, he'd reach out and make her look at him. Her attitude about everything, but especially him, made him batshit crazy. Not that he wanted her pining over him, but hell, he cared more about her than he thought he could ever care again.

He wanted to laugh out loud.

He'd never told her that.

"But it wasn't a one-night stand. We care about each other and I don't like you reducing what happened to something so meaningless," he said.

"Why are we hashing this out at eight thousand feet when we've discussed it before?" she asked.

"Because maybe I have a bit of regret."

"Excuse me?" Her voice screeched. "What the hell does that mean? I thought you said you'd never regret being—"

He took his hand off the control for a second, covering her mouth. "I sometimes think maybe I made a mistake by not giving us a chance." Shit. Not exactly how he expected to say those words, and especially not while flying an expensive plane he didn't own. He'd planned on telling her that tonight over dinner, since he'd tricked her into thinking there was a gathering at his place when, in reality, it was just the two of them.

"If you think that is going to get me to land this plane, well, the answer is still… oh, fuck it, hand over the controls."

"Are you changing the subject?"

"Hell yes," she said, glaring at him. "We're friends. Not lovers. Not boyfriend-girlfriend. Just friends."

He didn't like the sound of that, but he switched the controls to her side of the plane. "She's all yours." He flipped the comms switch. "Riley Tower, this is Booker requesting landing permission."

"Booker, this is Riley Tower. Permission is granted. Come in east to west for landing."

"You have to circle—"

"I know," she said, turning the plane three degrees to the left so she could come around the runway from the east.

Duncan smiled. "Let me know if you need a hand." He eased back in his seat and tried not to stare at her too much while she masterfully brought the plane to the runway, landing it with the precision of a sniper. The aircraft barely bounced as she skidded to a stop.

She followed the ground crew to a spot near the small aircraft hangar. They went through the shutdown checklist for the next ten minutes before jumping from the plane.

He tossed both their rucksacks over his shoulder.

"I can carry my own," she balked.

"I know you can." But he would be the gentleman his mother raised him to be. He tossed them in the trunk of the Charger he'd rented. Nothing like a good old-fashioned muscle car. Glancing at his phone, he opened the passenger door for Chastity. "Shit, nothing from Darius yet."

He tucked his phone in his back pocket and blocked the entry to the vehicle.

She tipped her head, staring up at him, eyes blinking.

He reached out, tucking a stray strand of blond hair behind her ear. Screw being a gentleman. Gently, he brushed his lips over hers in a sweet and tender kiss. It wasn't overtly sexual, but a promise of something more.

Something real.

Her hands rested on his chest, and he half expected her to push him away. When she didn't, he took that as a sign he could deepen the kiss. Circling his arms around her back, he pulled her tight. He could get drunk on her kisses. For an entire month, he told himself lie after lie about why he couldn't be with her, but at that moment, there wasn't a single one that made sense.

"Duncan," she whispered. "What are you doing?"

"Trying to tell you I made a horrible mistake walking away from you. I'm sorry. I can't stop thinking about you and what happened between us. I'd like to give us a try. I've given it some serious thought. You know I got burned—"

She patted his chest. "I know some chick broke

your heart, but I have no idea why. What the hell did Robin do?"

What a fucking loaded question, and did he dare tell her the truth?

"Does it really matter?" Most of the time, when he thought about Robin and what she did, his chest would tighten with a combination of the most excruciating pain and raw anger. However, over the course of the last few days, thanks to some serious soul-searching, those emotions lifted from his body.

"You say you made a mistake and want to give us a shot. Well, before I'm willing to do that, I need to know what happened. If you can't tell me, there is no way we could ever be anything but friends and co-workers."

"She was pregnant but decided it was too soon, so she had an abortion." Wow. He wasn't sure he'd ever said those words aloud, except to Buddy over a year ago when he'd found out. Buddy had been the best friend a man could ever ask for. He never judged, lectured, or even interjected his thoughts. He sat and listened and was there for Duncan. They even became roommates until Buddy fell hard for Kaelie.

Literally.

Chastity gasped, covering her mouth. Her blue

eyes grew wide, then narrowed into tiny slits. Fire erupted from them like a volcano. "Without talking to you?" she asked in a faint whisper.

He nodded. He might not have followed the church doctrine as his parents did, but abortion wasn't something he believed in. At least not for him, and especially with the woman he loved and wanted to marry.

Only Robin hadn't loved him.

But it was Robin not wanting to get married that threw him over the edge.

And he could have even understood not getting married right away, even though his parents would have lost their shit, but he could have done it, easily.

However, Robin took away any choice they had, and their relationship ended because of it. Over a year later, he'd come to understand that Robin wasn't the right woman for him. They didn't have the same core beliefs, and she wanted his money more than she wanted him—a cold, cruel fact he had to learn to live with.

"Duncan, I'm sorry."

"It gets worse."

"How?"

"It might not have been mine." That had been the toughest pill to swallow. At first, he thought perhaps Robin was just being cruel by tossing an affair in his face, but as it turned out, the baby could have been someone else's, and that fact nearly killed him.

"Fuck," Chastity muttered. "She's one cold bitch."

Though entirely inappropriate, he laughed. Not just at what Chastity said, but swear words sounded so innocent and sweet coming out of her mouth for some odd reason, and it eased the anger that filled his heart every time he thought about what Robin had done.

"That she is, but now I have a question for you." He took her chin between her thumb and forefinger. "What about Todd? It seems he's always around. I mean, he moved to Florida to be with you."

"And he moved back to Ohio two months ago."

"He did?" That was news to Duncan.

"He's seeing someone else. Actually, everyone is waiting for them to get married."

And that brought Duncan to the fear he told himself was driving him away from Chastity.

"I heard he proposed to you a while ago," he said. Marriage, kids, the white picket fence with a couple of dogs and maybe a cat or two was all he'd ever wanted. Well, besides being a fireman.

He'd given up on all of that the day he left Robin. But Chastity made his heart burn with desire again and for an instant, he thought maybe he could have it all.

"He did, but I didn't love him, and he knew it. He kept thinking I'd grow to love him. He moved to Florida after I broke up with him, hoping to win me over, but I finally got through to him and he went home."

"Wait. What?" He stepped back, scratching his head. "You introduced him at a few parties as your boyfriend."

"No. I didn't. That's how he introduced himself."

"Seriously? That's a little stalkerish, but you never corrected him."

"Oh, trust me, I corrected him plenty. He finally gave up months ago when I told him I hooked up with you."

"We didn't hook up till last month," he said, taking a long breath.

"I lied to him. I know. That's bad, but I needed him to understand he was better off with someone who actually loved him."

He smiled. "But we did hook up, didn't we?"

Once again, she patted his chest. "We had sex. But I should thank you for helping get through to him that he and I were never going to happen."

"I can't believe I didn't know he wasn't your boyfriend this entire time. God, I'm clueless."

"You're not clueless. You're just still reeling from what the bitch did to you."

He cupped Chastity's cheek, drawing her in for a single, but sweet kiss. "I'm past that and when this is over, I'd like to see where this might go."

"I'll need to think about it." She pushed past him and slipped into the passenger seat.

He tapped his aching heart. "Ouch."

Chastity rubbed her hands together, hoping Duncan didn't notice her body trembling like an earthquake. She'd always prided herself on being cool under pressure. It's how she survived firefighter school as a woman and being around Duncan in general. Her entire life, acting as if, or faking it till you make it, had been her only coping mechanism, and right now, she worried Duncan may have destroyed it in a tiny, but powerful kiss.

"Grab my phone. It's vibrating." Duncan lifted his ass cheek, exposing his buns of steel. Every day she was surrounded by hot firemen, but none of them were anywhere near as sexy as Duncan. Even on his worst day, he was hotter than sin with his chiseled abs, perfectly styled hair, tanned skin, and deep orbs that commanded one's attention.

"Looks like an email from Darius."

"Open it."

"I need the passcode."

"It's 242784," he said.

"I never use numbers, always go by the alphabet. So, this would be"—she tapped at the keypad—"*C-H-A-S-T-I...*" She let the last letter trail off as she dropped the phone to her lap. Her eyes blinked wildly as she stared at his profile going in and out of focus. "That's the beginning of my name," she stated the obvious.

"Really? Huh." He turned his head and smiled.

With shaky fingers, she picked up the phone and cleared her throat, deciding it had to be a coincidence. "Shall I read it?"

"Please do."

She did her best to ignore her thumping heart.

"Hey, Duncan,

Joey Richards is twenty. He's from Walnut Creek, but

he's a bit of a drifter. He's been picked up for dealing and spent the night in county lockup a few times for writing bad checks.

Chastity glanced over the phone. "Who writes checks these days?"

"Don't your parents?"

"We're Mennonites, not the Amish. We live in the modern world and use much of the technology it offers."

"So, your dad doesn't have this long beard?"

"He has a beard, but no, nothing like that."

"Good to know. Keep reading," Duncan said.

"He's also been arrested for a few bar brawls and possession of illegal substances. His last known employer is a mechanic shop up near Akron, but I can't find current employment for the last nine months. I have found some pictures of him hanging out with the Rossini boys, sons of Gandolfi Rossini who is currently spending life in prison for human trafficking."

"Fucking wonderful," she muttered.

"Wow. You just like swearing, don't you?"

She laughed nervously, understanding he was trying to lighten the mood. "The first time I said fuck, it was like licking the bowl after my mom made brownies."

"It doesn't even sound like a bad word when you say it."

"That's not what my mother said."

He reached out and squeezed her knee. His gentle touch comforted her aching soul, and right now, she needed to draw on his strength.

"Anything else?" he asked.

"Just that he'll be in touch."

He laced his fingers through hers. "You okay?"

"No. I'm not." She pointed. "Take the next right." Cornfields reached toward the sky with their stalky ends. A slight breeze sent them swaying back and forth in a seductive dance. A cow and horse pasture, filled with the finest animals, lined the left side of the road. Miles and miles of her family farmland stretched on for as far as the eye could see. It amazed her that her father could take care of the farm and be the local doctor.

"We'll find your sister."

"It's not just that."

"What is it, then?" The car jerked over a few potholes. The large white farmhouse that she'd called home for her first eighteen years came into view around a bend. Her father's older model Chevy station wagon graced the driveway.

"First, you should know my father is a doctor."

"What kind of doctor?" he asked with a crinkled forehead.

It reminded her of a cute little baby pug. "He's a general practitioner. Think Doc Baker on *Little House on the Prairie*."

Duncan scratched the back of his neck. "I have no idea what that is."

She laughed. Of course he didn't. The show was older than dirt and geared toward young girls. "He treats everyone in our church for basic ailments, does physicals, helps deliver babies, and encourages specialists when someone is really sick."

"Does he do house calls?"

"Yes. Dark ages, I know." She laughed, though quickly subdued the noise and cleared her throat. "There is something else I need to tell you."

"That sounds ominous."

It could be, depending on how he decided to take this little tidbit. "My mother might think you're my boyfriend." She closed her eyes, tight. It had been a stupid thing to tell her folks she'd been dating, but hell, they, too, had prayed God would help bring her to love Todd. She figured if they believed she had a man in her life, they'd give up on the idea that Todd could be the one who got away.

Duncan coughed, taking the turn into her

parents' home a little too tight, stirring up pebbles. "Say what?"

"I'm sorry," she said. "But ever since Todd came home and started dating the girl who works at my mom's family store, my parents have been on my case, and it shut them up, sort of."

"How long have we been dating?" The car came to an abrupt stop. "Just so I can get the story straight."

"Since last month." She blinked open her eyes and gasped.

His mouth was only a couple of inches away. He licked his full lips. "What do they know about me?"

She leaned back, but he cupped her neck, drawing her closer.

"I don't want to mess it up for you, so you should tell me before we go in," he said with a teasing tone. But his bourbon eyes conveyed a sincerity that made her melt like a chocolate bar in the hot sun.

"Just that you come from a long line of military men and that before you were a firefighter, you were in the Air Force. I might have mentioned that you're a nice Christian boy."

His moist breath tickled her skin, sending warm

pulses to the places he'd played like a harp that glorious night.

"I'm nice, but I'm no boy," he teased. "Do they know how old I am? Will that be a problem?"

"Yeah, they know and I can't say it pleased them," she whispered. Her chest tightened, and her muscles turned to putty.

His mouth hovered centimeters from hers. His gaze dipped between her lips and eyes.

"Duncan?"

"Yeah," he whispered.

"Are you going to kiss me?" She held her breath, not understanding why she'd asked the silly question or why she needed to feel his skin on hers. Comfort. That's all it was. The need to feel connected to another human. "Or do I need to do everything?"

He slipped his tongue between her lips. An audible groan filled her mouth as she wrapped her arms around his strong shoulders. Her fingers dug into his thick muscles. The smell of strawberries filled the inside of the car, making her dizzy.

Tap, tap.

She jumped, turning her head, coming face-to-face with her baby sister, Lilly, who stood with her face scrunched against the window, giggling. Her bonnet covered her long blond hair. She danced in a circle with her blue floral dress twirling around her skinny body. At eleven, she was still so pure and innocent. Part of Chastity had to appreciate the lifestyle to which she'd been born just for that reason.

"She's cute," Duncan mused.

But Chastity focused on her father as he stepped from the front door. He stood tall at six-two and had an intimidating, broad frame. At fifty, he looked fitter than most men half his age. His curly dark hair touched the collar of his blue button-down shirt. His beard, trimmed short, was dotted with gray hair. His turquoise eyes caught the sun, making them a sharper green that commanded respect.

People who didn't know her father might be terrified of him, but he was really a big old teddy bear. Loving, kind, generous, and always the voice of reason. His family had lived more in the modern world than her mother's and it had caused some friction in the family, but as the years went on, she believed her mother had seen that the twenty-first century wasn't as horrible as she thought.

"Is that your father?" Duncan asked.

"That's him."

"He's not much older than me."

"About the same age difference as we are."

"I think I'll drop you off here and go find a hotel," Duncan said with a slight tremble to his voice.

She laughed. "His bark is worse than his bite."

"I doubt that, and he thinks I'm your much older boyfriend?"

Lilly lifted her dress and raced up the porch steps. "I saw them kissing!"

"Shit, I'm a dead man walking."

7

Duncan had met many a father over the years, and no single one intimidated him like Dr. Jade. Duncan had no idea what it was about the man that made him want to run and hide under a rock like a little boy who'd just sloshed mud all over the house, besides the fact that Duncan had friends about the same age.

He sucked in a deep breath and held out his hand. "Dr. Jade," he said, hoping his tone sounded confident and worthy of being the man for Chastity in her father's eyes.

"You must be Duncan. Thanks for bringing my daughter home." Dr. Jade gripped his hand, perhaps a little too firmly.

Duncan did his best not to wince. "My pleasure and I'll do whatever it takes to find Serenity."

Lilly had jumped up on Chastity, wrapping her legs around her waist. "How long are you home for?" she asked.

"I only have a couple days off work." Chastity gave her sister a butterfly kiss.

Duncan smiled, remembering his mother doing the very same thing every night after bedtime prayers.

"We might be able to get a few more if we need them," Duncan added, and quickly wished he hadn't when Chastity glared at him.

"Lilly, why don't you go get some tea and some of Mom's banana nut muffins," Dr. Jade said.

"Sure thing, Daddy." Lilly raced off into the house, letting the front screen door slam shut.

Her father offered one of the rocking chairs and Duncan eased back, squirming a little as Chastity sat down next to him, with her father next to her, his emerald orbs eyeing him suspiciously.

Duncan couldn't blame the man.

"I can't believe how much she's grown since I was home last," Chastity said.

"I'm just glad she's still daddy's little girl. I'm

dreading when she blossoms into a young woman," her father said, wiping his brow.

"It happens to all of us," Chastity said.

"Well, you wait. Someday you two will have kids—"

"Dad. We've been dating a month. Really."

Duncan felt his cheeks heat, remembering the two times they had been together. Their naked bodies tangled up against her counter.

And then in his bed.

Hearing her call out his name as she orgasmed in his mouth. Nothing had ever felt so right as being with her, but he'd screwed that up.

And if he didn't get his mind out of her pants, he'd end up making an ass out of himself in front of her parents.

"Chastity tells us your family's roots are actually Quaker."

"Well, my great-grandparents were Quakers. My grandfather received a recommendation for the Air Force Academy and left, though he never really left the church. My dad also went to the Academy, met my mom, who is Lutheran, and that's how I was raised."

"You still go to church?" her father asked.

"Dad, can we save the twenty questions, please?"

"It's okay. I don't mind," Duncan said, taking in a deep breath. From the get-go, his religious upbringing had been a bone of contention with Robin. He didn't expect her to believe, but he at least wanted her to respect his family and their lifestyle. Answering her father's questions was the least he could do to help ease the man's mind.

Even if he was the fake boyfriend right now, it was something he intended to remedy.

"My work often prevents me from attending every Sunday, but it doesn't prevent me from staying close to my roots or having a relationship with God." His mother would be gushing with pride if she'd heard him. She'd always worried he'd become hardened, but truth be told, religion and God gave him a sense of being grounded. A purpose bigger than himself. "Chastity and I have gone a few times together." That hadn't been a lie, and he'd been grateful for her company.

Chastity's thick lashes fluttered over her blue-green eyes as she folded her hands in her lap. It wasn't a gesture of shame or even embarrassment. More like sweet innocence. She glanced up and smiled.

"I'm grateful that she had someone to go with," her father said.

Duncan let out a long breath. His heart thumped unevenly in his chest.

"Did you know Lilly wants to be a firefighter like her big sister? There was a fire in town last week while we were all there, and Lilly couldn't wait to go talk with the firemen," Dr. Jade said with a sense of pride as he puffed out his chest.

"I bet that really upset Mom," Chastity said.

"Actually, she told Lilly that she thought it was a great idea if maybe she stayed close to home to do it."

"You've got to be kidding me," Chastity said with her mouth gaping open. "Mom is encouraging such a male-dominated profession for her little girl?"

Duncan couldn't help but smile. It was rare that anything shocked Chastity, and he enjoyed how her sweet eyes grew wide with surprise.

"Your mother is very proud of you. Neither of us liked how you did it, but we're trying to be a little more supportive of Lilly and her dreams. She's so much like you that it's uncanny. She's not afraid to be herself, and honestly, that's a breath of fresh air after dealing with Serenity. She's so busy trying to shock us that she's never had the chance to find herself."

"Dr. Jade—"

"You're a grown man—older man—who happens to be dating my daughter. While I appreciate the gesture of respect, please call me George."

"George," Duncan said, swallowing, trying not to cough on the word *dating*. "Chastity told me a little bit about what is going on, and we've got a friend helping us who is a former member of Delta Force and is the best at finding people. He's already got some information on the young man you believe Serenity left with."

George ran a hand down his face, scratching at his beard before bringing his thumb and forefinger together at the tip. "We thought what Chastity went through was some serious rebelling, but Chastity was never disrespectful. She did everything she was supposed to do. She got good grades, did her chores, worked the farm or at the store. She just had dreams that weren't part of our lifestyle and we didn't listen."

"And I up and left in the middle of the night, setting a bad example," Chastity said.

"You did what you had to, and we know now that we were wrong in trying to get you to be something you're not." George's eyes glazed over. "Just a few months ago, Serenity said she wanted to be a lawyer. We decided we needed to encourage that, and then she met Joey and things got worse."

"It's not your fault," Chastity said, leaning over and resting her hand over her father's.

"It's hard not to blame ourselves for Serenity's problems. For not seeing them soon enough."

"I spoke to Serenity before she met that jerk, and it was just normal teenage angst. I think she was scared she wouldn't get into college or that you wouldn't let her live on campus. When I talked to her last month, after she started dating Joey, she barely even spoke of college."

Duncan glanced around the farm that stretched on forever. It was a beautiful piece of land, something he had no concept of growing up north of New York City, except for the few summers he'd spent in Lake George. But otherwise, his youth was filled with houses on top of one another, street ball, and he never lacked for a neighbor to play with.

It was both good and bad because half the neighborhood was nothing but trouble. The other half, like him, was trying to walk that fine line between being good and being a kid.

He imagined this lifestyle was both good and bad as well.

"I forbade her from seeing that man, and she thought it was just because he wasn't a Mennonite, but he'd been busted selling drugs to kids near the school."

"Dad, you did the right thing there. What our friend found out isn't good," Chastity said.

"That doesn't make me feel better." George continued to finger his beard.

"Someone want to open the door, please?" Lilly yelled, breaking the growing tension and fear that filled the air like a thick fog.

Duncan leaped from his seat, helping the young girl with a tray filled with a pitcher, glasses, and muffins that smelled as if they just came out of the oven.

His mouth watered.

"He's handsome," Lilly said, giggling in her sister's ear.

"Yes, he is," Chastity whispered.

Her smile sucker-punched Duncan. He took a sip of the sweet tea, glancing down the road as a brown SUV came into sight.

"Here's your mother." George pointed down the long windy driveway.

"Mom is driving?" Chastity's voice screeched.

"You haven't been home for a while," her father said with a tinge of a smile. "Things change."

"I can't believe it." Chastity rocked back and forth on the rocking chair with her little sister on her lap. "When did she get her license?"

"About a year ago, but it's only been in the last six months that she's been going off alone."

"Go, Mom," Chastity said, pushing her sister off her lap. She stood, took one step, and tripped, though Duncan had no idea on what.

Her arms flapped about wildly.

He reached out to catch her, but it was too late. She face-planted on the porch with a thud and a groan.

George burst out laughing.

Lilly plopped on the wood floor beside her sister, brushing back her hair. "I hope you don't do that when you fight fires. That would be bad."

"You okay?" Duncan asked, trying to bite back a laugh.

"I'm fine," Chastity muttered. "Just another day on the farm."

A tall boy—no, man—no, wait—a boy, stepped from the vehicle. He looked just like George, only scrawny, sort of. His hair was lighter, and he had no beard, but he was still a force.

"Hey look, it's klutzbutt," the boy said, pointing. He wore a short-sleeved blue button-down shirt with dark slacks.

"Don't call your sister that." A woman with long blond hair, much like Chastity's, emerged from the driver's seat. She wore a modest, long plaid dress. She carried herself with style and grace.

"Well, she is a klutz," the boy said, jogging up the stairs, carrying a couple of bags. He dropped them by the door.

"Doesn't mean you should call her names," George said. "Duncan, this is my youngest son, Neal, and my beautiful bride, Laurie."

"Nice to meet you both, though I'm sorry for the circumstances." Duncan helped Chastity to her feet, looping his arm around her waist, resisting the urge to kiss her.

Laurie pulled Chastity in and hugged her tight. She squeezed her eyes closed, and Duncan wondered if she would ever let go.

"So, you're the guy my sister is dating these days? I should warn you, she falls down a lot," Neal said. "Like all the time. It's embarrassing. For all of us."

"I know. We had a birthday party for one of our co-workers, and she face-planted right into the cake."

"Classic klutzbutt." Neal laughed.

"Neal Michael Jade. What have I told you about picking on your sisters?" George said with a stern voice that made Duncan stand up straighter.

"Sorry, sir," Neal said.

"Why don't you and Lilly go out to the barn and finish your chores." George pointed to the barn.

"Now?" Neal protested.

"Now," George repeated.

Neal took Lilly by the hand and scoffed off down the porch steps.

"How old do you think Duncan is?" Lilly whispered.

"Close to forty," Neal said.

"Stop that whispering. It's not nice." George planted his hands on his hips. "Sorry about that, but it's a question we're all wondering."

"Dad, really?" Chastity lifted her chin off her mother's shoulder. "That's rude."

Duncan swallowed. "I'm almost thirty-nine."

"I'll try not to hold that against you," George muttered.

8

"You look different."

Chastity stepped from her mother's embrace and swallowed. Her mother had always been able to read her emotions and sense the changes her body underwent. Two days before she'd gotten her period for the first time, her mother entered her bedroom with a box of various sanitary women's products. While her parents were old-fashioned as hell, they did have all the necessary talks with their children, often to the point of embarrassment.

"I can't put my finger on it, but something has changed," her mother said, holding Chastity by her biceps, rubbing her soft, motherly hands up and down. "Maybe it's this man?"

"Enough with pushing Duncan and me, okay?"

"I'm not pushing." Her mother narrowed her eyes, tilting her head, as if she peered into Chastity's brain, plucking out the fact she was pregnant. "But you sounded so excited about him when we last spoke," her mother said as if Duncan wasn't even standing across the porch.

Chastity stole a glance in his direction. He had shoved his hands into his pockets, his chin lowered, but his gaze was all on her as if he was trying to figure out what her mother had meant.

"Laurie, it's one thing to make our daughter blush, but something else entirely to make her boyfriend uncomfortable, who happens to be a guest in our home."

"Like you didn't just do that by asking his age," Chastity said.

Her mother kissed Chastity's cheek. "He's quite handsome," she whispered, hopefully so softly that Duncan didn't hear.

Poor man must feel like a slab of beef at this point.

"I don't mean to be so forward, but do you mind if I go through Serenity's room? We want to head over to Joey's last known address before it gets too dark." Leave it to Duncan to get right down to business and, thankfully, change the damn subject.

"Not at all," her father said. "Honey, why don't we let them search, since we've already done so."

"And you found nothing?" Chastity felt a sudden sense of nausea. She gripped Duncan's forearm for support. There weren't too many hiding places in their bedrooms. They had no doors on their closets. Not because of lack of trust; the house had just always been that way. There was only one bathroom upstairs, and all five kids had to share.

Her mother shook her head, sniffling. "I shouldn't have yelled at her."

"Ma don't do that to yourself. Serenity had no right to treat you and Dad like she has been."

"I don't know where I went wrong with—"

"Don't talk like that." Instinctively, Chastity covered her stomach. A mother's role was to love and protect, teach and lead by example. Her parents walked the same line they talked. There was nothing fake about them, and they were always loving and kind, even when they had to discipline their children.

Just a little on the rigid side and overbearing,

but thinking about the life growing inside her belly, Chastity could actually understand why.

"You did nothing wrong, and we'll find Serenity and hopefully talk some sense into her," Chastity said.

"You're a good child." Her mother cupped Chastity's cheek and gave it a good pat. "It's getting close to the dinner hour. I'll go make you some sandwiches for the road. I've also made up Manly's old room for Duncan."

"Thanks." Chastity took Duncan by the hand and led him quietly through the foyer, down the hall, and up the one staircase near the kitchen. Their parents had taken down the dated wallpaper and finally painted the walls various earth tones that she'd picked out years ago. Light browns, tans, a russet red in the dining room, a mustard yellow in the kitchen, and as she passed her old bedroom, she had to do a double take.

"What is it?"

"My parents finally painted my room a light green. I'd always wanted a green room instead of the floral wallpaper I'd grown up with."

"You had a room full of flowers?" He peeked his head into her room. "I have a hard time believing you were a little girl who played with dolls."

She laughed. "I had dolls, but I didn't really play with them, unless it was to scare the crap out of my brother Manly. He was scared of his own shadow, and I made one of my dolls into a bad version of Chucky."

"Wonderful, now I'm going to have nightmares about a crazy doll and that movie about children and some cornfield." Duncan tugged her hand.

She glanced down at their intertwined fingers and let out a nervous laugh. "I can't believe you're afraid of horror movies but handled my parents and their embarrassing questions." They watched many movies together over the last year, but Duncan was nowhere to be found when anyone picked a horror flick.

"Trust me, I was shaking worse than when we had that fatal car crash last month. Your father scares the shit out of me, and I'm terrified they both hate me, and not just because I'm an old man."

"You're not that old." She laughed. "Right now, they think you're the best thing since sliced bread."

"Maybe, but that could all change in a flash, and then I'll be running naked through the cornfield while your father hunts me down with a shotgun."

She patted his shoulder. "You have nothing to worry about." Only, she had no idea how her parents would take her news.

But she wasn't going to tell them this visit, and she had to tell Duncan first.

"Where's your sister's room?" he asked.

"Next door on the right." She pushed past him and stepped into Serenity's room. It looked exactly the same as she remembered. The walls were a pale yellow and the bedspread was white with floral-accented pillow shams. A pink stuffed elephant sat proudly on the bed. Her sister had won that at a local carnival where she had to hit three balloons with a dart from twenty paces away. She'd been only seven and beat out everyone in the family, including their dad, who still swears he didn't let her win.

Chastity didn't believe him.

"Serenity didn't go anywhere overnight without this." Chastity sat on the edge of the bed and squeezed the elephant. While Serenity didn't like boyish games, she enjoyed that carnival game because it made her the center of attention for the rest of the night, something Serenity craved all the time.

"She's seventeen now, and if she ran off with that boy, I doubt she'd be bringing a stuffed animal."

"Perhaps you're right." She and Serenity were like night and day. Where Chastity had always been a tomboy, Serenity was into makeup, hair, and used to sneak regular clothing under her traditional Mennonite dress. It was highly frowned upon for women to wear anything but plain dresses, but like most things, times were changing, and more and more young girls and boys wore more stylish clothes, though still quite modest.

Serenity always tried to push the envelope.

"Mind if I go through her closet?"

"Go right ahead." Chastity set the elephant on the bed before going through her sister's drawers. A pang of guilt glided across her heart. It felt like she was breaking some sister code by rifling through her things. Her clothes were that of a typical young Mennonite lady with a few jeans, blouses, and other regular clothing dabbled in.

Satisfied there were no clues in the dresser, Chastity pulled back the quilt and lifted the mattress. "Bingo," she said, snagging what appeared to be a scrapbook or journal. "Exactly where I hid mine. We always had to make our own beds, so it was the one place I knew my parents would never look."

"I don't want to tell you what I hid under there."

She chuckled. "I can only imagine." She'll never forget the first time she'd seen a dirty magazine her first week in firefighting school. Her fellow fire-fighters hadn't meant to leave them lying around the break room. She didn't know who blushed more, her or the young men in the station.

With shaky fingers, she flipped open the book.

Duncan sat next to her. His one hand pressed into the bed behind her back, the other one a little too close to her bare thigh.

The first few pages were from when she was younger, so Chastity flipped to the end, where she used the pages as a journal over a place to display images with crafty sayings and cute paper cutouts. She focused on the page written the day before she left home.

"I really thought he loved me. Honestly, truly loved me. I read through my other entries about him, and it reminds me

of how sweet he could be. He promised to take me away from all this. He even said he'd take me to see my sister, Chastity, the wonder daughter. The daughter my parents are proud of, even though she ran off in the middle of the night, defying their wishes."

Duncan's fingers curled around her shoulder. "Don't take that to heart."

"Kind of hard not to. I've always known Serenity was jealous of me, but it's the same with our brothers. Serenity always felt like the only way to get noticed in this family was to rebel." Growing up in Chastity and Manly's shadows couldn't have been easy. The male and female perfect children, only Chastity had to stumble her way back into her parents' good graces by proving she had the chops and the faith to follow her dreams.

Only what was Serenity's dream? It seemed Serenity never thought past being the center of attention and that tugged at Chastity's heartstrings.

"What else does it say?" Duncan asked.

"But Chastity didn't do it wrong. She'd done everything right until she became a firefighter, which is girl-power badass. I wish I had realized that a long time ago. It might have saved me a broken heart.

Joey doesn't even know I know yet, but tomorrow, I'm

going to confront him and tell him he can go off with one of the other girls he's been seeing and telling lies to.

Mom and Dad are actually encouraging this law school stuff, and maybe they're serious about letting me stay on campus. Chastity is right. I have to get my shit together, and it starts with saying goodbye to Joey.

Until the next time…"

"That was the last entry," Chastity said, closing the book. "I've got a bad feeling about this."

"I wish I could lie to you and tell you I felt differently, but it sounds like she had every intention of breaking it off with this Joey guy."

"And she was going to confront him." Chastity chomped down on her fingernail. There had been nothing to believe that Joey was violent. All the information they had about his criminal record hadn't shown any evidence of a temper.

"I need to call Darius and see if we can get a location on Joey. We should leave now," Duncan said.

She breathed in slowly through her nose, exhaling through her mouth. She repeated that another five times, doing her best to remain calm. Every alarm bell in her head rang at full blast.

Her sister could be dead.

"Chastity?" Duncan tilted her chin up with his thumb and forefinger. "Chastity?"

"What?" She blinked a few times, but her eyes wouldn't focus. "I'm fine," she muttered, continuing with her controlled breathing.

"Relax, sweetheart. We're going to find her."

"You can't promise that we'll find her alive."

"Don't talk like that," Duncan said, cupping her cheeks and lowering his eyes to catch her gaze. "We need to have a little faith in the man upstairs."

She opened her mouth, but before she could utter a single syllable, he kissed her with his warm, tantalizing lips. He satisfied a thirst that she had deep in her throat. She was going to have to tell him soon about the baby. She had no right to keep that information from him. Whatever happened going forward, he needed to be part of the equation.

Her parents might have gotten over her leaving in the middle of the night, but having a child out of wedlock, with a man who didn't love her, that made her a harlot.

The sound of heavy footsteps echoed from down the hallway, but that didn't stop Duncan from deepening the kiss, wrapping his arms around her body, drawing her tight.

She pressed her hands against his chest and pulled back just as her father came into her peripheral view, but he stepped back and cleared his throat.

"Duncan," she whispered.

He took her hands in his and brought her to a standing position. "Let's go find your sister."

9

Duncan had spent the last ten minutes listening to Chastity read through the rest of Serenity's journal. She'd been head over heels in love with this Joey kid. Hell, he wasn't a kid at twenty and probably severely hardened by his time in jail. He'd manipulated Serenity and her need for attention. Joey knew exactly what to say to get Serenity to follow him to the ends of the world. Duncan just hoped they'd be able to find the couple and, more importantly, that Serenity was unharmed.

He had serious doubts about that. However, he couldn't let Chastity or her family know that's how he felt. Chastity needed him to be her rock, and he could give her that. The need to protect and care for her came as naturally to him as running into a burning building.

He fought his feelings for her tooth and nail and now he regretted not letting his love for this woman blossom while they discovered and explored each other. He didn't need a lot of time with her to know she was the one.

His mother always told him that when the right one came along, it would be both terrifying and joyful. He never understood that love could be such a sharp contrast, but that's exactly how he felt about Chastity.

He rolled the Charger to a stop in front of a double-wide in a trailer park just outside the town limits of Walnut Creek.

"Let me do all the talking and asking of questions, okay?" The anger seeping from Chastity's body filled the air like thick smoke choking and burning his lungs. He couldn't let her go off on anyone they might speak to or they'd never find Serenity, and time was of the essence.

"I can't promise I'll keep my mouth closed."

"At least I know you'll try." The pavement crumbled under his boots. He took his sunglasses off, shoving them in his breast pocket. He'd worn a pale-blue button-down shirt out of respect for her parents' lifestyle. The jeans didn't really fit in as most men wore black slacks, but it was close enough.

An older man wearing a jean vest with chains dangling everywhere stepped from the trailer. He wore a red bandana, and both arms were lined with tats. The right was dedicated to a bald eagle and the American flag, while the left had an image of a woman with long hair and an ominous smile.

"Can I help you?" the man asked, folding his thick arms over his broad chest.

"We're looking for Joey Richards."

"That's my son. What do you want with him?" The man broadened his stance.

Duncan took that as an act of quiet aggression. "He's been seeing my friend's little sister."

"The Mennonite girl, right?"

"Yes. And she's missing," Duncan said, holding Chastity's hand with a little more strength than necessary. He wasn't sure if he was the one squeezing or if it was her with the death grip, but he supposed it didn't matter.

The man took in a deep breath and let it out slowly. "I kicked my son out a couple of weeks ago."

"Why?" Duncan asked.

"Not that it's any of your business, but he was

freeloading, and I won't have it. He's a grown man and capable of work. If he can't live by my rules in my home, he can go find another place to live."

"When was the last time you saw him?" Duncan asked.

"A couple of days ago. He said he got a job as a mechanic up in Canton and already found a place to live."

"Do you know the name of the auto shop?" Duncan wasn't sure if he believed this man or not. But right now, he had no choice.

"Putter Auto. I already told the police all this."

Duncan arched a brow and stole a glance at Chastity. "When were they by?"

"Two days ago. They were asking about the girl, whom I never met. I didn't even know he'd been seeing anyone." The man relaxed his stance. "I'm sorry she's missing, and I truly hope you find her. If I knew more, I'd tell you and the police."

Duncan handed the man his card. "If you hear from him, can you give me a call?"

"Will do."

Duncan tugged at Chastity's hand, but she dug her heels into the ground.

"I didn't get your name," Chastity said.

But Darius had given them Joey's father name,

so Duncan wasn't sure why she was asking, but he decided to let her have a crack at it.

"It's Lester."

"Lester," she started, "did Joey leave anything behind?"

"Some clothes. I told him he had one month to get them all. If not, I'd donate them. I don't think he's coming back for them since he called me a jerk of a father when he left."

"Do you mind if we take a look at them? Look inside his room?" Chastity asked.

Duncan inched closer, slipping his hand from hers and wrapping his arm around her waist, bracing for Lester to tell them to take a hike. The intel Darius had given them about Joey's father wasn't much better than his son. Though it had been years since he'd been picked up for anything and he'd supposedly turned over a new leaf.

The jury was still out.

"Are you related to the girl who's missing?" Lester asked as he rubbed the side of his scruffy face.

"She's my little sister." Chastity's voice quivered.

Lester nodded. "All right. Come on in."

Duncan blew out a long breath as he followed Chastity and Lester into the trailer. As mobile homes go, it was spacious with a large family room. A dark-brown sofa was pushed up against the wall under a window that looked out over the backyard. A blue recliner with a handmade afghan tossed across it separated the family room from the kitchen.

"Anyone else live here?" Duncan asked as Lester pushed back one of the bedroom doors.

"Just me."

Duncan leaned against the doorjamb, watching Chastity look under the bed, in the closet, and open and close the dresser drawers, shoving what few contents were inside around.

"What are you looking for?" According to the journal, Serenity had been inside this trailer at least once, if not more.

"I have no idea, but maybe she left something behind, or he did." Chastity glanced up. "I don't believe Joey just got a job and moved my sister there. When Serenity is done with something, she's done and all she wanted to do was confront him for using her and cheating on her."

"I already sent Darius and Timothy the name of the auto shop. The Aegis Network happens to have a guy in the area. Dylan Sarich. He'll stop in and see what's what. If Joey is there, we'll drive up tonight. If not, we'll stay at your folks and regroup in the morning."

"I can't sit around and do nothing." Chastity planted her hands on her hips and stared.

Duncan swallowed. He understood her restlessness, but they had only one lead, and his buddy happened to be in Canton for something else and said he'd stop by. He was closer, and it made more sense.

"I want to talk to some of her friends, but they might be more apt to talk with you," Duncan said.

Chastity rubbed her eyes, looking the other way.

"Come on. Let's get out of here. If we hear that Joey is in Canton, I'll turn the car around and drive like a madman to get you there. I promise."

Chastity nodded, taking the hand he offered. One thing he wished more than anything was to be able to hold her in his arms all night. It wasn't about sex right now; he just wanted to comfort her. Be there for her.

Be her rock.

Be the man she relied on.

Shit, he really was head over heels in love with her, and they hadn't even had a single date. His mother always told him that when it was right, he'd know it.

Well, he'd tried to run from it, and that had gotten him nowhere.

"Thank you for your time." Duncan shook Lester's hand.

"My son is a lot of things, but I don't think he'd hurt that girl."

Duncan led Chastity back to the car, where he tucked her in the passenger seat. He could feel the tension seeping from her skin. He had a sister, and he couldn't imagine what it might be like to know she could have been kidnapped, or even just run away with a deadbeat guy.

Duncan pulled out of the trailer park and headed back toward the farm.

"Why don't you check my phone?" He pulled it from his back pocket and rested it on her thigh. He thought if she had something to focus on, it might change her mood.

She tapped the keypad and scrolled through his texts and emails.

"Nothing."

"We'll hear something soon." He gunned the muscle car as he entered the highway. He'd always been a bit of an adrenaline junkie, but the older he got, the more he only wanted to settle down and have a family. He'd watched many of his co-workers find the love of their lives and ride off into the sunset.

Could he have that with Chastity?

"Can I ask you something?" She shifted in the seat, facing him.

"Of course."

"It couldn't be a coincidence that your passcode is the beginning of my name. So, why'd you make it that? And when?"

He gripped the steering wheel. Butterflies danced in his stomach as if he were in middle school and trying to steal his first kiss.

The only question that remained was whether he would be truthful.

Screw it. If he wanted a chance, he had to be.

"Remember Rex and Tilly's big party a few months ago?"

"You mean the one where I fell down the stairs and took you out with me?"

He laughed at the memory of him trying to catch her before she face-planted on the floor, only she ended up with her face in his chest and her legs around his waist.

It was a really nice feeling, even if it had thrown his back out.

"Do you remember me kissing you?"

"I wasn't drunk, so yeah, I remember. But then things got all awkward again."

"I thought you were still hung up on your ex," he admitted. "But it was that night that I changed my passcode, and I've been kind of stuck on you since."

"You have a weird way of showing it."

His heart lurched to his throat. "I know and I'm sorry about that. I want us to try our hand at dating." Jeez, he sounded like a total moron.

She let out a dry laugh. "I'm not sure how to take that, but we need to talk about some things."

"What things?"

She leaned over, checking out the dashboard. "This isn't something that should be talked about at eighty miles an hour."

"Now you're freaking me out." Either she was going to tell him no way in hell would she date him because that ship had sailed. Or something entirely worse, though he couldn't figure out what that could be. "There, I eased up on the gas, so what's on your mind?"

"I was just messing with you." She punched his shoulder. "Sometimes it's too easy."

He didn't believe her for a second, but he wasn't about to push.

10

He wanted to date her?

They were way past dating. They were going to be parents. Shit. She wasn't ready for this. It didn't matter that she wanted it more than anything. She had planned on falling in love, getting married… then having babies.

She slipped from her bed and tiptoed across the hallway toward Manly's old room. Her parents had, hopefully, gone to bed. But all she wanted to do was talk. Taking in a deep breath, she tapped on the door. "Duncan?" she whispered. "Can I come in?" She lowered her gaze, realizing she was wearing one of his shirts she'd snagged after they'd gone for a run and she'd spilled coffee on it. It had become her pajamas and she'd tossed it in her suitcase without thinking.

Shit.

The door squeaked open.

She gasped, staring at Duncan who wore nothing but boxers. His thick thighs bulged with tight muscles. His tanned skin glistened in the moonlight that filtered through the window.

And his hair was still perfectly styled.

She reached out and ran her fingers through his thick mane. It never felt like he had any product in it, but something had to make the strands go in different directions.

"What is it with you and your need to mess up my hair?" he asked as he quietly closed the door behind her.

"It's always so perfect. Too perfect."

"You're perfect," he whispered, tugging her to his chest. His lips brushed against hers with gentle but firm pressure. "I've been looking for this shirt."

His skin sizzled under the touch of her fingertips.

"Stop," she said as she took two steps backward, putting some needed distance between them. "My parents are right down the hall. They're light sleepers, and my father owns a shotgun."

Duncan held up his hands.

"Besides, we need to talk." She wasn't sure she could do this while he was in just his underwear, but she couldn't wait another day. Another hour. Minute. Second. It was making her batshit crazy.

"All right." He took her by the hand and led her to the queen-sized bed.

That wasn't going to make this easier.

He helped her onto the bed, actually pulling back the covers, and eased her between the sheets.

"I'm not sleeping here with you," she said so softly she wasn't sure he could hear as he climbed in, tucking himself under the comforter and fluffing the pillows.

"I don't expect you to. Besides, your father would probably have me hung if he found us. I was just a little cold."

"It's not my father you should worry about, but my mother. She'd hang you by your balls herself."

He squirmed, yanking the covers to his chin. "Please, don't talk like that and have your mother in the same sentence. It's rude."

"Sometimes you crack me up." She shifted to her side, resting her head on her hand, which was propped up by her elbow. "You're an oxymoron filled with contradiction."

"Now you've just attacked my manhood in a different way."

She slapped his shoulder playfully. "You know what I mean. Both our lives are filled with Christian values, and we both still go to church and believe in a higher power, yet we don't follow any of the doctrine."

"And your point?" He rolled to the side and rested his hand on her hip.

While she worried her parents might walk in at any second, it felt so right to lie next to him.

She shivered.

"What's going on?" he asked, pulling her closer. His warm breath tickled the skin on her lips. He smelled like a combination of peppermint and pine.

His thumb and forefinger pinched her chin as he tilted her head, kissing her before she ever got the chance to answer his question. A deep groan bubbled through her throat. She caved to her desire and leaned closer, wrapping her arms around his muscular body. His soft skin singed her fingertips.

But the more she avoided telling him, the harder it would be.

She splayed her hand over his chest and pushed. "We really need to talk about what happened."

"What is there to talk about? I said I was sorry

about how I behaved, and I want a second chance. You still care about me, right?" He had the nerve to wink.

"I need you to be serious." Over the last year, she'd learned that Duncan often skirted issues when they might cause him emotional pain. She could understand that to a certain extent, but right now, she needed him to listen with an open mind and heart.

"Are you going to shoot me down and make me crash and burn?" he asked, cocking his head.

"No." She palmed his cheek. "But what I'm about to tell you will change things drastically."

"How so?" He narrowed his eyes.

Her heart thumped in her throat, making it difficult to swallow. "The night we were together after Buddy's wedding. And again the next morning."

"What about it?" He brushed a piece of her hair behind her shoulder.

She bit back the tears that threatened to break free and turned her head, not wanting to look him in the eye.

"My birth control failed," she stated matter-of-factly, blinking her eyes.

He reached out, tipping her head. "What are

you saying?" His russet orbs narrowed, then grew wide. "Are you pregnant?"

"Yesterday, before I showed up at your house, I took a home test, and it was positive."

He shoved a finger in his ear and wiggled. "I don't think I heard you correctly because we can't be having a baby."

"But we are."

"Holy shit," he mumbled as he ripped off the covers and jumped from the bed. He ran a hand through his hair, which he only did when he took off his hard hat after a fire or got out of the shower at the station before he styled it. His hair was his obsession. "This is not what I expected you wanted to discuss."

"You haven't thought that it might be possible?" Her pulse pounded in her ears.

"I honestly didn't give it any thought. I suppose I should have, but I didn't." He stopped at the foot of the bed, hands on his hips, staring.

She held the sheets to her chin, gripping tightly. Her lungs burned with every breath. Telling him in her parents' home while everyone was sleeping felt like a manipulation. And maybe it was because if he yelled, they'd come running and she didn't think he wanted that.

"You're sure you're pregnant?"

"Well, I haven't been to the doctor, but I'm a week late, and the stick I peed on gave me one big old plus sign."

"Wow," he mumbled as he sat on the edge of the bed. "Wait a second. This is going to sound like the biggest asshole remark, but I thought you were on the pill. I mean, I've seen that little pill box at the station."

She cocked a brow. "I just told you, it failed."

"Yeah, I guess it did," he said with a slight chuckle.

"Not something to laugh at. Why are you not shocked?" Nor did he respond in a way she imagined.

"Oh, trust me, I am. I'm just not sure what to think or feel right now. I'm kind of numb. When I left you that night, I was more concerned about hurting your feelings and protecting my heart than realizing I hadn't used a condom. Same thing the next morning."

"If you were so concerned about my feelings, why did you leave the way you did?" She bit down on her tongue. Not only was the comment accusatory but it was said with more venom than she'd intended.

"Fear," he said. "But it wasn't so much about being afraid of you as it was knowing how I felt about you."

"How do you feel? About me and about me being pregnant?" She held her breath as he climbed back on the bed and slipped between the sheets once again.

"I could rattle off a dozen emotions that I feel right now, but that doesn't deal with the situation." He rolled to his side, taking her in his arms.

She thought about squirming away, but it felt good pressed against his chest, staring into his dark, sweet eyes as if she belonged in this spot. "Please. I need to know what you're thinking."

He kissed her nose. "I'm thinking you need to make a doctor's appointment and we have some long discussions ahead of us, but it doesn't change the fact that I want to date you."

She buried her face in his neck and started laughing so hard she not only worried she'd snort, but that it would wake up the entire house.

"Why is that funny?"

"I have no idea, but it beats crying."

Duncan's body stiffened. "You know I want you to have this baby. I mean, I don't believe in abortions."

"Neither do I, so it's not something I'm considering." She swallowed her laughter as it turned into a guttural sob. "I don't expect anything from you."

"Well, I'm not walking away, but I honestly don't know what to do next, and I think we need to focus on your sister."

"Thank you." She rolled her feet to the floor. He hadn't responded like she thought he might with demands of marriage, and that was a relief, but part of her wanted a declaration of love, or something.

He grabbed her and pulled her back to the bed. "I don't want you to go just yet, okay?"

"You're confusing me," she whispered as he tucked her backside into his chest, his knees tucked up against hers.

"I don't mean to. I care about you more than I've let on, and that alone scares me. A baby freaks me right the fuck out. The fact that it's with you?" He kissed her temple, snuggling in closer. "I think I'm in shock."

She let out a long breath and closed her eyes tight. She had no idea what any of this meant or where it would take them, but at least she'd told him the truth.

All she needed to do now was leave this bedroom before she fell asleep.

11

Duncan blinked his eyes open. The morning sun peeked into the room, warming his face, but it was the body sprawled out over his chest that heated his skin and charred his heart.

Or maybe she mended his heart.

He'd gotten Chastity pregnant, and he feared she might not be ready. She was only twenty-six, and they hadn't had any romantic relationship. Sure, he knew he loved her, but he had serious doubts about her feelings. Add in a baby, with her religious background, and he worried that everything she did going forward would be driven by what she thought she was supposed to do.

He needed to know—to believe—that she wanted to be with him, even if there wasn't a baby.

He wasn't sure that was an answer he could find.

Her long blond hair covered his chest. Her arm rested over his stomach, her knee between his legs, reminding his body how they made a little person in the first place. Spending the night with her was simply torture, so why had he held her so tight?

The answer was twofold. He needed to hold her like he should have that night. That was for him. But he also needed to show her he did indeed care very deeply and for whatever reason, he thought this might do exactly that.

Chastity moaned as she arched her back, brushing her hair from her face. "You let me fall asleep," she mumbled, rolling to her back, but he pulled her to his chest again. He wasn't ready to let go.

He might never be ready.

"What time is it?" she asked.

"Almost six."

"Oh my God." She covered her face. "My parents have been up for at least an hour, and I'm sure my mom went into my room. She was notorious for peeking in while we slept."

"I think all parents are guilty of that. I really hope no one opened my door."

Chastity nuzzled her face into his neck. "I don't think even my mother would do that to a stranger. Of course, if she couldn't find me, who knows? I mean, my sister is missing. My mom is a little on edge."

"That reminds me." He reached over her body, snagging his phone from the nightstand and unlocking it. "Darius has sent a few emails. Why don't you read them while I use the little boys' room?"

"You're seriously going to leave me here?"

"The damage is already done."

"Fine."

The cool floor did nothing to reduce the heat burning in his loins. He wanted her more than he wanted anything in his life. After hiking up his jeans, he poked his head out into the hallway before making a mad dash to the bathroom.

Quietly, he closed the door, turned the lock, and slapped cold water on his face. He braced his hands on the sides of the sink and stared at his reflection in the mirror.

He was going to be a father. He should be happy. Thrilled. Excited. Yet all he could do was recoil inside his soul. Besides the things that could go wrong in the first trimester, he couldn't shake the sadness that Robin carved into his heart. The deception and betrayal cut way too deep, and he resented that feeling. He didn't want to shout from the rooftops about his and Chastity's news—good news—because they needed time to be a couple first.

Only, he kept backpedaling, and he had to stop. He had nothing to fear. Chastity was sweet and kind. She was everything any man could ever hope for, and he'd be the dumbest asshole if he let her slip through his fingers.

"Duncan!" her voice screeched through the door as she pounded on it. "Let me in."

"What's wrong?" He yanked open the door.

She shoved him, hard. His back slammed against the wall as she skidded across the floor, dropped to her knees in front of the toilet, and vomited.

He bent over and pulled back her hair, rubbing her back.

She gagged and retched for another good three minutes before flushing the toilet and rolling from her knees to her butt. "That's something I never wanted you to see."

"What, morning sickness? I hear it happens to a lot of women."

"Excuse me," her mother's voice bounced between his ears.

He let out a long breath before glancing toward the hallway.

"Did I hear you say morning sickness?" her mother asked, clutching her middle.

Duncan sat on the floor, holding Chastity in his arms, while she buried her face in his bare chest.

Her mother stared at them with big eyes, her hands clasped together as if in prayer.

He mentally barraged himself for not closing the door. Had he done that, maybe her mother wouldn't have overheard. But even with the cat out of the bag, it wasn't his place to confirm or deny the coming of a child.

"Chastity?"

"Ma, I think I might be sick again." She shifted from him to the porcelain bowl. "Can we discuss this later?"

Her body trembled and lurched.

"Sure," her mother said, reaching in and taking the knob in her hand. She nodded briefly at Duncan, then closed the door.

He hadn't expected her mother to let that go.

No, he actually worried she might come back with a shotgun and a preacher.

His own mother was going to have his head, and he didn't think he'd survive the lecture his father would give him.

But even that would be better than holding Chastity in his arms on the bathroom floor after she suffered from morning sickness—in front of her mother.

"That came on so quickly. I mean, I felt like shit yesterday morning, but I didn't get sick. I took one step out of bed, and bam, my stomach started smacking my throat."

"When my sister was pregnant, she said one day it started, and just as quickly, one day, it stopped." He helped her to a standing position. "It won't be like this forever."

Tears lined her sky-blue eyes. "My mother sounded so disappointed."

"She didn't look that way. She appeared more shocked and concerned than anything else." He swallowed. Not a good way to make a positive impression on your girlfriend's parents.

Girlfriend.

Was that what Chastity was? God, he hoped so.

"I can't deal with this right now. I need to get out of here. I only got to read a few lines from Darius' message, stating that Joey isn't in Canton, but he's got a lead in Columbus and said Dylan was on his way there."

"Let me jump in the shower real quick, and then I'll meet you outside and we can leave. Is there a back staircase in this place? I'd prefer not to run into either of your parents right now."

"You and me both," she said, pulling her hair back. "Right now, I only want to focus on finding my sister. Then we can deal with this." She placed her hands protectively over her belly.

He sucked in a quick breath. His lungs burned, and he couldn't fill them with enough oxygen. His gaze zoomed in on her womb. His knees buckled, and he had to hold on to the sink in fear he might fall over.

"You okay?" she asked.

"I think I have morning sickness."

"Oh no, you don't. You don't get to go there." She waggled her finger. "I understand that this is a lot for you. We had two great sexual encounters and we find ourselves in a situation, but you don't get to pretend to feel sick."

"I'm not." He placed his hand over her stomach. "We're really going to have a baby?" Flashes of holding pudgy little fingers in his hand as he and a toddler walked across the beach flooded his mind. He'd had this vision a dozen times, but he never saw Chastity waving from a chair with her toes in the sand like he did now.

She covered his hand with hers. "Yes. We are. But I wonder if I should have waited to tell you until after we found my sister."

"That would have made me angrier."

"You're angry?" she asked.

"I'm a little annoyed that you didn't come to me when you realized you were late and that you could indeed be pregnant." Annoyed wasn't the correct word, and it was directed at himself, not her. Only he did wish he could have offered her a shoulder to lean on while she waited to find out.

"And tell you what? We weren't a couple and why worry you until I knew for sure."

He frowned. It might be a logical answer, but with this kind of life situation, emotion trumped logic every day of the week.

"I'd like for you to tell me everything that has to do with the baby, please?"

She cupped his face. "I won't keep any of that from you, ever. I promise. But I really need to focus on my sister and not this. Can you do that for me?"

"I can." He would part the Red Sea for her if he could.

12

Chastity squared her shoulders as she stepped into the large kitchen. The butcher-block-style table, which sat at least twelve when flipped open, had fresh-cut tulips placed in a crystal bowl right in the center. As a child, she always loved being in the kitchen, only not to cook because she hadn't been given her mother's talent or passion for it, but just for the rich smells of family suppers.

Her mother stood before the stove, flipping what Chastity hoped would be her mom's famous homemade buttermilk pancakes. The sizzle of the batter hitting the skillet made her mouth water.

"That smells wonderful," Chastity said, realizing how hungry she'd suddenly become. She glanced around for her younger brother and sister, but they were nowhere to be found. Neither was her father or Duncan.

"Pancakes always helped me with morning sickness. Only thing I could eat in the morning the first few months."

"I remember." Chastity loved babies ever since she was a little girl and with each new sibling, she did her best to help her mother with feedings, diaper changing, and more importantly, playing with her little brothers and sisters. She might have been a tomboy, always getting dirty, playing rough, and doing things associated with little boys, but she loved children. Her lips curved into a smile at the memory of teaching Serenity, the girliest of the girls, how to pee properly in the woods, making sure she never touched poison ivy. Neither Serenity nor Chastity's parents were too thrilled.

Chastity filled a mug with steaming hot coffee. The aroma hit her nose, sending her stomach sloshing again. She pushed it aside.

"I didn't like coffee much either and never got my taste back for it after you were born."

Chastity blinked, staring at her mother's back. She imagined tears streaming down her face and disappointment etched into every crinkle of her forehead.

"Ma. I'm sorry you had to find out that way."

Her mother flipped a couple of pancakes before putting them on a plate and turning. There were no tears, no signs of anger, or any other emotion that went along with shame. "I didn't mean to invade your privacy, but you sounded so desperate as you called for Duncan and banged on the door. I had to know what upset you so much."

"Well, as you now know, I wasn't upset, just about to barf." She snagged one of the pancakes and broke it apart, popping a piece between her lips. The fluffy treat melted in her mouth, immediately calming her stomach.

Her mother tossed the spatula in the sink. "But I sense you're not thrilled about having this baby, which concerns me."

"I just found out yesterday and Duncan last night, so we're both still a little bit in shock. Obviously, this wasn't planned."

Her mother folded her arms. She almost always wore the traditional Mennonite attire of a long, plain dress. She occasionally wore slacks when working in the fields, but that was rare. Chastity wished her mother would spread her wings a little wider. She understood her mom would never leave the community, which was fine, but her ma was the smartest woman Chastity had ever known. She resented the submissiveness of women in the Mennonite culture. Her father never treated her mother as if she were less than him. Actually, it was quite the opposite. He joked that his wife was the boss, and the secret to a happy marriage was saying 'yes, dear' as often as possible. That usually, his wife was always right about things. But that wasn't entirely true. Her parents' marriage was a partnership, something Chastity wanted desperately.

"Do you love him?" her mother asked, taking off her apron and hanging it on the rack near the sink. Her tone was tight and filled with worry but not a drop of disdain.

That only confused Chastity.

"I do," she admitted, staring into her mother's warm sea-blue eyes. They emitted love, kindness, and understanding, something she didn't think her mother could give her under these circumstances.

But her mother constantly surprised her.

"Thing is, I don't know if he loves me," Chastity said, biting her lower lip. She couldn't tell her mother that she and Duncan had only one night and one morning together before he walked out of her love life, saying her friendship had been more important to him.

That hurt and part of her worried that was all she'd ever be to him.

A good friend.

Well, and the mother to his child.

"I see." Her mother blinked her eyes, clasping her hands together as if she were about to pray. "It's obvious to me he cares deeply for you and your child. Have you told him how you feel?"

"No. The relationship is still new."

Her mother hugged her middle and let out a long breath.

"I'm sorry I've disappointed you, Ma."

Her mother raced across the kitchen and wrapped her loving arms around Chastity. "Oh, honey, you haven't disappointed me. Not at all. I might be old-fashioned and think marriage should come before children, and to be totally honest, I'm so grateful to hear you say you're going to have this baby." She stepped back, cupping Chastity's cheeks. "You're twenty-six years old and have proven you can make it in this world, and I'm so proud of the woman you've become. You know, I didn't realize what a fool I've been until I saw you and your young man this morning. You're a good woman with strong principles. I won't lecture you or try to push my beliefs on you. I have faith you and Duncan will do right by each other and this baby, even if it's not in the conventional way."

But Chastity wanted convention. She wanted to wear a white dress, which made her laugh out loud. She'd probably trip on it as she walked down the aisle. Still, she wanted to be the bride, then the wife, and finally the mother. She wouldn't give up her job, no way in hell. She loved being a firefighter.

Having it all was something she knew she could do, and no one was going to stop her.

"That means the world to me." She kissed her mother's cheek. "I never meant to hurt you when I left. I didn't want to leave the family; I just wanted a chance to chase my dreams."

"I understand all that now," her mother said, pulling back a chair and setting the plate of pancakes on the table.

Chastity sat down and dug in, her body demanding nourishment, her stomach craving heavy starches. Normally, she had a protein shake for breakfast right before her jog, but hell, pancakes, or maybe waffles, she figured, would become her go-to meal for the next few months.

"You'll understand soon enough, but as a

mother, I had my own hopes pinned on my children. You showed me that I need to support my children's dreams, not my own. Only your sister, Serenity, doesn't seem to have a dream other than to screw up her life."

"We found a journal in her room." Chastity stuffed more food in her mouth, closing her eyes, trying not to moan as she chewed and swallowed.

"What?" Her mother settled into a chair. "Where? What did it say?"

"Under the mattress and Serenity wasn't as far off the beaten path as you think. She wants to be loved, and she's looking for it in all the wrong places. Duncan is confident this new information is right on the money."

"What new information?" her mother asked.

This was where she needed to lie, making her a little squirrely, but it was for the best. Her mother had enough on her plate. "His buddy found Joey, and he's watching him right now."

"And your sister? She's there? Is she okay?"

Chastity swallowed. "They haven't seen her, but we believe so, yes."

Her mother slumped back in her chair. "I have a bad feeling about this. I saw something in that boy's eyes that made me afraid for Serenity. I didn't trust him."

"We'll find her and bring her home." Chastity wanted to promise, but she couldn't go that far out on a limb. This morning, they'd found out that it was highly probable that Joey was involved in a human trafficking ring, which meant the worst for her sister.

Her mother nodded, picking at her pancake. "I put too much pressure on Serenity to be more like you. I drove her away. I drove all of you away."

Chastity rested her hand on her mother's shoulder. "Ma. Stop. You did what you thought was best, and I love you for it. I'm who I am today because of you, Dad, and the lifestyle you raised me in. Honestly, I wouldn't be able to deal with being pregnant had you not given me the tools to be my own woman while following the path God has for me."

"You're going to make a great mother." Her mom nodded, wiping away her tears.

"God, I hope so."

"And Duncan is going to make for a good father. I will pray that the two of you work things out and get married. I think you're perfect for one another."

Chastity wanted that too, but she had to deal with one thing at a time. "Where is Duncan?"

"He and Dad took their breakfast outside."

Chastity dropped her head to the table with a resounding thud. "Dad is going to scare the shit out of Duncan. He's probably sitting there with a shotgun next to him."

"I haven't told your father about the baby, and I won't until you're ready."

Chastity snapped to an upright position. "You'll keep that from Daddy?"

"For now. Remember, he's a little more open-minded than I am, so don't worry about it. We will support you no matter what."

"Thanks, Ma." Chastity reached out, covering her mother's hand. "I should get going. I'll call you when we get to Columbus."

"I made some snacks and sandwiches. Let me put them in a small cooler. I'll bring them out in a couple of minutes." Her mother thought food was the answer to every question, but in this case, having some of her homemade favorite foods made her stomach happy.

She made her way toward the front door. She saw her father and Duncan sitting on the porch through the big picture window. Their backs were to her, so she couldn't see their expressions, but they both rocked back and forth in the chairs.

There didn't appear to be any tension, but she could imagine what those two were talking about.

"I can't tell you how much Laurie and I appreciate you and your friends helping to find Chastity's sister."

Duncan set his plate, which he had to resist licking clean, on the end table and lifted his coffee mug. "We're a tight crew and we never leave a man, or woman, hanging."

"Is that all this is with you and my daughter?"

Duncan gagged on his hot coffee. "No, sir." He pounded his chest with his fist and swallowed. "While she's one of my team, I care more about her and in a different way." Wow. He sounded like a buffoon. "What I'm trying to say is I care a great deal for your daughter."

"It shows." George raised his leg, resting his ankle on his knee, rocking back and forth. "As her father, I feel I should warn you that Chastity is a strong, stubborn woman and fiercely independent."

Duncan let out a slight laugh, trying to remain

respectful. "I'm well aware. She's the only woman on the crew and at first, I think we all tried to lighten her load. She quickly put us all in our place."

"I bet she did. She was always a handful, but in a good way. I knew she'd leave, but her mother hoped Chastity would settle down into this way of life. It's not an easy one."

"Neither is being a female firefighter, but Chastity is one of the best." Duncan's pulse raced, and a little sweatband beaded across his forehead.

"You speak with pride." George turned his head. "I only want my girl to be happy and being a firefighter makes her smile, but being with you seems to be the icing on the cake."

Duncan took in a deep breath, letting it out slowly. He assumed, based on the conversation, that George had yet to hear about the baby. Duncan hoped he'd still be in her father's good graces when he found out.

"I speak the truth." Duncan nodded.

"I believe that about you," George said, shifting in his seat. "So, please don't hold back your thoughts, feelings, or any information you have about Serenity. I don't think she walked away from this farm on her own accord."

"Why do you say that?" Duncan was thrilled to be off the subject of him and Chastity. He glanced over his shoulder. While he wouldn't lie to Chastity or her father, he worried how her mother would take the news, and he sure as hell didn't want the two younger children hearing it.

"Laurie would say she saw something in his eyes, but I found him completely disrespectful, and I didn't like how he tried to fit in as if he knew and understood our culture. It was so fake, and he had a subtle arrogance about him."

"My buddy has uncovered disturbing information about some of the people he's been hanging out with." Duncan stared out into the morning sun. Its rays stretched over the crops like long tentacles from a jellyfish floating in the ocean. It was almost as calming as the ocean.

"How disturbing?"

"Human trafficking, disturbing." Duncan held up his hand when George opened his mouth. "It doesn't mean he's involved."

"But it's a possibility."

"Yes, sir. My buddy has eyes on Joey and I have other friends poking around, not to mention my father is a JAG lawyer, and he's doing his own digging."

"You really do care about my daughter."

Duncan more than cared. He loved Chastity, but he needed to tell her before her father.

"Hey, you two," Chastity said with a bright smile as she inhaled the sweet floral scents of summer in Ohio. The sun heated her skin, wrapping her in a warm blanket. "You both look cozy."

"Just enjoying a fine morning and good conversation," her father said, raising his mug before taking a long sip.

Chastity's stomach sloshed as the bitter smell filled her nose.

"Duncan, have you heard anything more from Darius or Dylan?"

"Dylan has eyes on Joey, and Darius is working his magic. But we should get going." Duncan stood, his face tight like a terrified small boy. "I packed up our stuff, and it's in the car. I think I got everything of yours."

"Thanks. Mom is bringing out sandwiches for the trip." She tried not to smile as she glanced between her father and Duncan. Her father had been her hero her entire life. Duncan was the man of her dreams.

"I don't know how anyone in this family stays fit and trim with your mother's cooking," Duncan said.

"Yeah, well, don't get your hopes up. Chastity's a crappy cook," her father said.

"I know," Duncan readily agreed. "During overnight shifts, we all take turns cooking dinner. The one time Chastity did it, not only was it inedible, but she slipped on whatever it was she tried to make and sprained her wrist. We don't let her near the kitchen anymore."

Her father burst out in a big old belly laugh.

"I don't see what's so funny." She planted her hands on her hips and glared at her father and Duncan, who had joined her father in his fit of hysterics.

"I'm sorry, sweetheart, but you've always been such a klutz," her father said.

"Everywhere except when she's working. It's weird. She can't stand on her own two feet half the time without falling over, but under pressure, during an emergency, she's amazing," Duncan said as he puffed out his chest like the proudest man on the planet. "When it comes to fighting fires, I trust her with my life."

Her father's laughter halted. He stood, extending his hand. "You're a good man, Duncan. I look forward to getting to know you better."

"Me too, sir." Duncan nodded. "We best be on our way. We'll call as soon as we get there."

Chastity hugged her father.

"You picked a good man," her father whispered.

She swallowed the lump that had formed in her throat, making it hard to breathe. There was so much confusion and too many unanswered questions swirling around what might or might not be a relationship with Duncan. He kept saying he wanted to date her, but how the hell did you do that when a baby was in the picture? Dating implied dinners and long walks on the beach, not doctor visits, morning sickness, and picking out a crib.

Life had certainly given her quite a twist.

"We should be at the address Dylan gave us in half an hour."

Chastity's voice smacked Duncan's ears. If sound had a taste, hers would be powdered sugar with a splash of cinnamon over a sourdough friedcake. Even under stress, her voice had a sweetness to it that calmed his nerves.

"You just got a text from Dylan," she said.

"Read it to me." Duncan had learned from his father to never keep anything from the woman you loved, even if you thought you were protecting her from something terrible. So, Duncan made a deal with himself that he'd be honest with Chastity about everything he found regarding her sister.

So why did he find it impossible to tell her how he felt?

Even her father had suspected he held back his feelings. Boy, had that been a weird conversation. It was as if her dad knew he danced around on tiptoes because he was afraid to get hurt again.

That sounded pathetic.

"He's on the move. Driving a white Chevy pickup. Older model, but in good condition. I'm half a mile behind on Route 58, heading south near Buckeye Lake. He's got a girl with him, but it's not Serenity."

Duncan reached out and squeezed Chastity's leg. "We're going to find her," he said, projecting as much confidence as he could muster.

"You don't know that," she mumbled, flipping open the map. "We're following the north shore of Buckeye Lake," Chastity pointed out the window. "But he's on the southwest tip. If we stay on Route 79, we'll hit 58 in about six miles, and we can take that south."

Duncan pressed the gas pedal, hitting eighty in a fifty-five. He passed three cars before slowing down to sixty-five. They needed to get there quickly but getting pulled over for a speeding ticket would only slow them down.

"I'm going to do whatever it takes to bring your sister home."

She glanced in his direction. "Thank you for being here for me."

He nodded. The words 'I love you' formed in his mind. But this wasn't the time or place. "Text Dylan back."

"I'm just going to call him." Chastity hit the speaker button and waited three rings before Dylan picked up.

"Hey, Duncan, how far out are you?" Dylan's deep voice boomed out of the cell.

Duncan had met Dylan a couple of times when he'd first interviewed with the Aegis Network. Dylan was one of four brothers who worked for the Orlando branch of the organization.

"Duncan's too busy driving like an ass," Chastity said, holding on to the bar above her head as he once again weaved into the other lane to pass an eighteen-wheeler. "He should only be allowed in the cockpit of a plane."

"This must be Chastity," Dylan said with a hearty laugh.

"Yep. And we're about five minutes from Route 58."

"I just turned left onto Chautauqua Boulevard.

I will share my location with Duncan's phone so I don't need to keep texting. I'll let you know when we stop and where you should go to stay under the radar. We don't want to spook this kid."

"Any idea what he's doing? Or who this girl is?" Duncan asked. "And when did she show up?"

"First time I saw her was when he left the apartment with her a bit ago. I snapped a couple of pictures of the girl and sent them to Darius. She seemed kind of out of it. Either severely hungover or maybe drugged. She looks to be about the same age as Serenity."

"My sister's journal mentioned that she thought Joey had cheated on her with more than one girl," Chastity said.

"So far, this is the only girl I've seen him with."

"Thanks," Duncan said, gripping the steering wheel as he punched the gas once again to pass some slower vehicles. "Anything else we should know?"

"Yeah, but you won't like it," Dylan said.

Duncan laced his fingers through Chastity's, glancing in her direction.

Her normally confident blue eyes were wide with the fear of the unknown. He knew her concern for her sister was stressful enough, but add in the baby and the fact her mother had found out, and that had to be taking a toll.

And they hadn't really discussed much in the car. He tried, but Chastity wanted to wait until after they found her sister.

"Boyd Rossini is in town."

Duncan blinked while Chastity squeezed his hand so hard his fingers turned white.

"Has he had contact with Joey?" Duncan asked.

"Not that I've seen, but that doesn't mean anything."

"Then how do you know he's in town?" Chastity asked.

"Darius found a credit card trail. Turns out his uncle owns a place on Buckeye and the boys get a lot of gas at a marina on the lake. They might have been living here for a while, but considering the amount of money these two have, and they own more than one house in multiple states, who knows where they call home."

"What do we know about the uncle?" Chastity asked, tugging her hand away. She pulled out a notepad and pen. "Was he involved in the human trafficking case against Gandolfi?"

Duncan admired her composure and professionalism. If it had been his sister, he might be going ballistic right about now.

"None that anyone could prove, but he's on the FBI watch list, so they think he's up to something. Look, I better go. He's making another turn. I'll be in touch," Dylan said, then the phone went dead.

"Look in my phone for a guy named Chuck Wilson."

"Who's he?"

"A buddy of my dad. They went through the Academy together, and Chuck happens to work for the FBI. He might be able to get us some intel. I should have called him sooner."

"You called your dad?" she asked. She'd met his parents at Buddy and Harper's wedding. That night, she spent more time with them than she had with him. It was as if she'd given up on him altogether, which was part of why he followed her home that night.

"I thought he might be able to get information we couldn't."

"Thanks for doing that." She set the phone on her thigh, flipping the mode back to the Find My iPhone feature. She pointed to a street about five hundred feet away.

"Hello? Duncan?"

"Hey, Chuck, how are you?" Duncan tapped the brakes as the map indicated he needed to turn right.

Chastity pointed again to another street about half a mile away.

"I'm good, but I heard from your dad late last night. He told me your girlfriend's sister is missing?"

Duncan swallowed, glancing at Chastity, who gave him a puzzled expression with an arched brow.

"Yes. And we believe she got tangled up with a young man hanging around the Rossini brothers, and we just found out they have been at their uncle's all summer."

"You mean Anthony Gandolfi?"

"That's the one. I understand you can't give me any official information—"

"I'm going to cut you off there, son."

That interruption only served to send the acid in Duncan's stomach to his throat.

"I can't get into the details, but trust me when I say we've got eyes on him, and if things go my way, he'll be indicted soon."

"Can you tell me if he was in any way connected to the human trafficking that sent his brother away?" Duncan asked, taking a turn.

Chastity held up his phone, showing a message from Dylan.

"I'm sorry, Duncan, I can't comment. And I need you to stay clear of him."

"I can't promise that. If he has anything to do with the abduction of my girlfriend's sister, I won't back down. Nor will she."

"Fair enough," Chuck said. "I will contact our agent there and let him know what is going on. I'll send you his contact info. I'd appreciate it if you kept him and me informed. His name is Bo Ingalls."

"Will do. Thanks, Chuck."

"Hope to see you soon. And make sure you bring that girlfriend."

Chastity tapped the phone. "Dylan says to go to Ricki's Diner, which is right there. He's inside, and Joey is down that dirt road in some old house on the lake." She shifted in her seat. "Care to explain the girlfriend thing?"

If he wasn't mistaken, she tried not to smile, but the twinkle in her eye gave her away. "I called my dad yesterday from your folks' farm. They think I'm your boyfriend, so I figured my parents should think the same." He shoved the gearshift into park and leaned across the center console, tipping her chin up with his thumb and forefinger.

Her rosy, plump lips parted.

"Besides, we need to spend time together as a couple and see how we really feel about one another."

Her thick lashes fluttered and before she could protest, his tongue slipped into her mouth. The kiss came as a promise that he'd do whatever it took to show her how much he cared and wanted to be with her, even if there wasn't a baby.

Something he knew would be harder to prove, but he had to.

"Duncan," she whispered.

"What?"

"We should get inside. We can deal with all this later."

He cupped her face a little more harshly than he'd planned, but he needed to get his point across. "I care a great deal about you, Chastity. I made a mistake a month ago walking out of your house. I got spooked, and I'm sorry. It's not going to happen again."

She let out a long breath, circling her fingers around his wrists. "Thank you for that, but I can't deal with this until after I get my sister home."

He nodded. If he loved her as much as he thought he did, then giving her space while they searched for Serenity should be an easy thing to do.

14

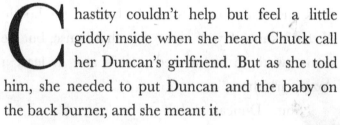

Chastity couldn't help but feel a little giddy inside when she heard Chuck call her Duncan's girlfriend. But as she told him, she needed to put Duncan and the baby on the back burner, and she meant it.

"Over there," Duncan pointed to a man sitting in a booth, drinking coffee and eating a piece of pie. "That's Dylan."

"He's nice on the eyes."

"Not only is he married, but I can be a jealous boyfriend." He rested his hand on her hip and kissed her cheek. "I hope I'm nice on your eyes."

"If you weren't, I wouldn't have slept with you," she admitted, inhaling his rich pine scent. "For the record, you're a hell of a lot sexier than that guy over there."

"Flattery will get you whatever you want." He led her through a maze of tables until they reached the diner's far end.

Dylan nodded. "Have a seat," he said. "I'm going to skip the pleasantries and get right down to business."

"I don't like the sound of that." Chastity swallowed. She took Duncan's hand and squeezed.

"I wish I had better news," Dylan said, leaning back and resting his arm on the back of the booth. "I don't know if your sister is in that house, but we do know there are armed guards and at least a dozen girls there."

"Shit," Duncan said.

"Why are we sitting here and not down by the house?" Chastity asked as her leg bounced up and down, rattling the table.

"Two of my brothers, Ramey and Logan, are here."

"When did they get here?" Duncan asked.

"I asked them to come in last night. I also contacted Buddy and Arthur, who contacted the rest of your crew. I'm not sure who is coming in, but we should have a good team assembled by nightfall, which will give us time to make a plan. We have to hope they don't try to move the girls before then."

"You called a bunch of firefighters?" Chastity asked, blinking. Sure, they were all ex-military, and some had even seen combat, but their role was to fight fires, whether on land, at sea, or even in the sky, not to carry out a sting operation.

"They're also special operators with the Aegis Network," Dylan said.

Duncan laughed. "You've heard all the stories about Arthur's wife and what went down at their marina."

"Yeah, and I helped fight that fire at Kaelie's when Buddy got burned, so I get we're all capable, but these men have families and—"

"We're about to have a family, and it's not going to stop us from going in," Duncan said with a tight jaw.

She kicked him under the table.

"Ouch. That hurt," he said with a scowl. "What the hell did you do that for?"

"No one knows that yet and I don't need anyone blabbing to the rest of our team."

"My lips are sealed," Dylan said.

"Thank you." She leaned back. "I'm sorry. But

I hate pulling everyone away from their wives and children."

"It's what we all do," Dylan said, holding up his mug. "When one of our own needs a little helping hand."

Her phone buzzed and so did Duncan's.

She yanked hers from her purse and stared at a group text. "Arthur, Kent, Buddy, Hawke, and Garth are all less than two hours away." She glanced at Duncan, catching his caring gaze. "None of them had to come."

"No offense, ma'am, but they all also work for the Aegis Network, and we called them in," Dylan said.

"If you got an SOS from any of them, what would you do?" Duncan asked.

"Yeah, yeah, yeah, I'd be here in a heartbeat," she said, setting her phone on the table. As the only woman on the team, she sometimes felt like the odd man out, even though none of her crew ever made her feel that way. The only one who had ever treated her differently had been Duncan.

Looking back on that now, she realized Duncan cared about her. That was the only thing that made sense in how he had treated her. One minute, the consummate gentleman; the next, just another one of the guys; and the next, flirting like there was no tomorrow. One thing she understood was the confusion of caring for someone whom you felt like you shouldn't and worried they didn't return the same feelings.

The waitress came by the table. "What can I get you folks?"

"I'll have a cheeseburger, fries, and a Coke," Duncan said, nudging her. "You should eat. You need some extra calories now."

Dylan coughed. "Dude. I have kids and my wife would have shot me if I ever said that to her while she was pregnant."

"I'll have the same," she said, glaring. The last thing she needed was for the world to know she was pregnant and then treat her like she was some little woman who needed coddling.

"I'll be right back with your drinks," the perky brunette said as she bounced away.

"So what else do we know?" Chastity asked. The idea that her sister could be held captive, perhaps beaten or even raped, sent a cold shiver across her body.

Duncan put his arm around her, squeezing her shoulder.

He was such a sweet and kind man. Even when

he acted weird in the last month, he still had a heart of gold. Their child was lucky to have him as a father.

"Ramey is still doing recon. Now that you two are here, I will head down to help him." Dylan slid a small envelope with a plastic key card across the table. "I've got two rooms down the street at the local inn. You two can have one to yourself. The rest of us will make do."

"You're leaving?" Chastity stared at him, ignoring the idea that she'd have a hotel room with Duncan while half her team hung out in the room next to them. The only one she'd talked to about Duncan had been Buddy, but only because he'd walked in on a conversation she'd had with Buddy's wife, Kaelie.

"We need to know exactly what we're dealing with, so we can make the best plan. I'll be back once we have more men here, so we can rotate eyes on the house while we develop a plan to get those girls out, and hopefully, your sister is one of them."

She reached out and grabbed his hand. "I know you don't know me from Adam but thank you."

"My pleasure." Dylan stood tall, tossing a twenty on the table, and strode out of the diner like he hadn't a care in the world.

She scooted to the other side of the booth. When she moved, she hadn't expected to be staring at Duncan, but now that she was, she couldn't tear her gaze away.

The waitress came, setting their food and drinks in front of them. Her stomach growled, but still, her eyes remained locked with his.

"I'm not ready for anyone on our team to know I'm pregnant, so could you please stop with the extra calories and shit?"

"Sorry, I didn't think." He dipped a fry into a hunk of ketchup before plopping it in his mouth. "I just worry about you and also, well, if I haven't told you, I do want to have this baby with you."

She wished she hadn't taken a sip of her soda as she coughed and gagged, and it ended up coming out of her nose.

"Shit," he muttered, handing her a bunch of napkins, but that didn't really help as she knocked over both their sodas, which landed right in her plate, and then her plate landed in her lap.

The waitress raced over with more towels.

Chastity's cheeks heated with embarrassment as she continued to cough while trying to down a glass of water.

"Can you just get us two orders to go and the bill?" Duncan asked.

"Sure thing," the waitress said.

Duncan made his way next to her, still cleaning up the mess she'd created.

Her coughing had subsided, but her mortification hadn't. "And this is why my family calls me klutzbutt."

"That was all me. My timing really sucked on that one." He patted down her jeans. "But I meant what I said. I know you want to put off talking about this, but we will be parents together, and I want a second chance. You haven't said no, but you haven't said yes, and that's shaking my confidence and honestly making me crazy."

She jerked her head. "You're incredibly overwhelming right now."

"I know. But you needed to know how I felt when you told me about the baby last night. I need to know now how you feel about me."

Her mouth dropped open, and she snapped it shut. Her mind went totally blank, but her heart fluttered and swelled with the kind of love a woman should share with her children's father.

"I like you," she mumbled, unable to say the

words she desperately wanted him to hear. "A lot and I want us to date too."

"I want more than that." He palmed her cheek, giving her a tender kiss on the lips. "A lot more."

"Slow down, please," she begged. While she wanted the world with him, her thoughts were somewhere else. "I promise, we can sit down and have this conversation after I get Serenity home."

"All right," he said, pressing his loving mouth against her cheek. "But I'm telling you now, I'm going to show you how much I care about you. That this isn't just about the baby."

"You don't know when to quit, do you?"

"I won't quit until you know just how much you mean to me. After that, if you don't want to be with me, well, then okay. But until then, I'm going to keep pushing."

15

D uncan had hoped for a little more alone time with Chastity, but their room soon filled with his crew and they needed a plan.

Logan sat at the desk, while Ramey and Dylan kept a watchful eye on the house.

Arthur leaned against the wall with his arms folded. Buddy stood next to him in the same position. If Duncan had a best friend, it would be Buddy, though all his brothers-in-arms were family.

Kent sat on the floor with Garth and Hawke. They were a few years younger than Duncan, but a few years older than Chastity, which meant she was the only peon in the group.

And that thought reminded him that she was

pregnant and only a couple months away from a desk job. He worried that might make her stir-crazy, but it would only be temporary, and he wasn't going to be the kind of husband—wow, did he just think that?

Well, he wouldn't be the man who stood in the way of his woman's dreams.

"Ramey says there are five armed men at every access point of the house and one on the roof," Logan said. "We don't know what's inside. However, I suspect we will soon."

"We need to take out the man on top first," Buddy said. "And that's not going to be easy. He's got one hell of a view of the property up there."

"Actually, if we create a diversion on the water, that will draw everyone's attention there, and we can come in from the back and flank them," Arthur said, rubbing his chin.

"Chastity and I will create the diversion." Duncan didn't want Chastity anywhere near this crazy plan, but he knew she wouldn't stay behind. He wouldn't say anything about her being pregnant in front of their crew, but he would plead with her once they were alone.

If they were ever alone.

"Buddy and I will come in from the east,"

Arthur said authoritatively. "Ramey and Dylan will come in from the west."

"Hawke, you take the back of the house. I don't think they'll take a man off that post even with a diversion," Buddy said.

"Once their men are on the move, I'll flank to the front and enter from the main door," Garth said.

"I think we have a solid plan." Arthur nodded. "Hawke and Garth, why don't you two go relieve Ramey and Dylan, so they can get an hour of shut-eye before we spring into action."

"Sure thing," Garth said, jumping to a standing position. At six foot four, Garth might be the tallest member of the crew.

"I think we need to go in earlier," Hawke said. Half the time, everyone called him 'Runt.' At five-nine, he was definitely the shortest, except Chastity.

"We stick with five in the morning unless you get wind they are on the move earlier." Buddy rubbed the back of his neck.

"I agree," Chastity said, pressing her leg against Duncan's on the sofa in a subtle gesture of affection.

He resisted the urge to pull her close. He knew

she'd push away with their co-workers in the same room and worse, she'd be mad at him.

"Keep your comms on," Arthur said.

"Will do." Garth pushed open the door, and Hawke followed him out. They were good men, and Duncan was grateful to have them involved in this mission.

Arthur pushed from the wall and stepped closer to the sofa. "This is a good plan. We'll nail these bastards and bring your sister home."

"I can't tell you what it means to me that you and everyone else came," Chastity said.

"We take care of our own," Buddy said as he slapped Arthur on the back. "Let's leave these two lovebirds alone."

Chastity coughed.

Duncan followed suit.

Buddy and Arthur's laughter echoed down the hall, even after they slammed the door shut.

"I didn't say anything about us, I swear." Duncan shifted, pulling her onto his lap.

Her arms looped over his shoulders and her hand went right through his hair. "Buddy overheard me talking to Kaelie a few weeks ago."

"Do they know about the—"

She covered his mouth with her palm. "No. I told

you I just found out right before my mom called about Serenity. I was confiding in Kaelie about the fact we slept together, and you acted like a jerk afterward."

"I'm going to be apologizing for that for the rest of my life, aren't I?"

She dropped her forehead to his and closed her eyes. "No. I understand why. But I feel like you only want to get back with me because of the baby."

"I'm sorry that's how you feel, but it's not true. I told you I wanted us to date before you dropped the bomb."

"Are you sure you weren't just being supportive and trying to be there for me when I told you Serenity was missing?"

"Open your eyes." He cupped her face as her lashes fluttered. "I have a confession to make."

"What's that?"

"There was no big get-together planned the other night at my place. I only invited you, and I was going to make homemade pizza and wings and try to seduce you with my witty charm. And if that didn't work, I would grovel on my hands and knees for a second chance."

"Seriously?"

He smiled at the way she bit down on her lower

lip, her eyes wide with surprise, a touch of desire, and a twinge of doubt.

Doubt he'd put there.

He picked her up and carried her across the room to the bed, laying her down gently, propping the pillows up behind her head before resting next to her sweet body. "I wasn't lying when I said our friendship means everything to me, only we go way deeper than that."

"You're irresistible when you get like this," she said.

He sprawled his hand over her tight belly, fanning his thumb gently before scooting down and lifting up her shirt, dabbing kisses on her warm skin. It was hard to believe that his baby was growing inside her.

"What are you doing?" she asked as her stomach quivered with a giggle.

He snapped his head up. "We have a couple of hours to kill, and no one will bother us."

"These walls are paper-thin. I can hear the television in the next room."

"Okay." He sat up, searching for the remote, and flipped the TV on, not caring about what was playing. "So, they will hear our television, and we'll just be quiet." He whipped his shirt off, tossing it to the floor.

She had crossed her ankles and put her hands behind her head. Seductive and gorgeous weren't even close to how she looked, smiling up at him with lust filling her ocean orbs.

"I can be quiet, but can you? I mean, you made this—"

He quickly shoved his tongue in her mouth. He really didn't want to be reminded of his near-howl of a month ago. He hadn't made that noise since the first time he'd had sex. It had built up in his throat, getting caught as he held his breath, trying to hold on to the moment for as long as he could.

It hadn't lasted nearly long enough the first time.

Or with her.

He hoped his performance would be a tad better the second time around, but it hadn't. He had no control when it came to Chasitity.

He wiggled her out of her shirt and bra like a horny teenager, their lips constantly finding each other in wild passion. He wanted to slow it down. To make it less desperate.

But holy hell, he desperately needed to be inside her.

Then she flipped him on his back, straddling him, staring at him with a wicked smile.

"Whoa," he mused as her tongue darted out of her mouth and down his chest, over his tight, sensitive nipple. He hissed.

That only made her do it again.

And again.

Her fingers glided down his stomach, and she easily popped open the button to his jeans. Before he could even think to protest, her hand firmly circled him, stroking slowly as she teased the tip with her tongue.

His toes curled as he pushed her hair to the side and watched as he disappeared into her hot mouth.

"Chastity," he said in a breathy moan.

She glanced up at him, lapping at the tip, letting her teeth graze his sensitive skin.

"Oh my God," he whispered. "You're driving me mad here."

Her lips quivered into a smile before her eyelids closed and she took all of him, gliding up and down, her hand following, adding more pressure.

He'd explode right there if he didn't stop her and catch his breath.

Tugging at her hair, he kicked his pants to the

floor and swiftly removed hers. "My turn," he whispered.

"Oh yeah," she said, rolling to her back, but she misjudged where she was on the bed and she flopped herself right off. "Shit," she mumbled as she hit the floor with a thud.

He tried not to laugh, but he couldn't help it.

"Are you okay?" He gave her a hand and pulled her into his arms.

"Just totally embarrassed." She brushed back her hair that had fallen over her flushed face. "Only I would fall out of bed in the middle of sex."

"I adore your klutziness," he said, tracing his forefinger across her lips, down her collarbone, and over her nipples.

He watched them tighten and pucker with the pleasure he brought them. Her breathing labored, and she arched her back.

Losing himself in her body, he tried to kiss every inch of her before settling between her legs. She tasted like bottled-up ocean air and honeysuckle. Her scent was more intoxicating than the strongest whiskey. He'd never stop wanting to please her in every way. He wanted to be the icing on her cake. As cheesy as it sounded, he wanted to complete her. To be her other half. To be the one man she could rely on for everything, but especially, he wanted to be the man she thought of before she went to bed at night and the first thing she thought of in the morning.

Lord knew she was all he could think about.

"So beautiful," he said against her. Her fingers threaded in his hair, pulling him closer. Her hips rolled with his touch.

Her soft moans grew louder and deeper. She tossed her head back and forth, her nails digging into his scalp.

"Duncan," she cried out, probably a little too loudly.

But he loved hearing his name tumble out of her mouth as she was on the verge of climaxing.

He licked and sucked and teased, wanting to make her scream her passion. But she covered her face with a pillow and muffled the sweet sounds.

Her body jerked and twitched as he kissed his way across her stomach, tossing the pillow aside and pressing his erection against her.

"Oh God, yes," she begged, wrapping her legs around his waist and guiding him deep inside.

He groaned.

"This might get loud." He covered her mouth with a ferocious kiss, hoping that would silence them both, but with every thrust, the headboard hit the wall. "You've got to be fucking kidding me," he whispered, pulling her lower on the bed.

"If they didn't hear me before, they sure as hell heard that." She buried her head in his neck, grinding her hips.

But again, the damn headboard thumped against the wall.

"Screw the bed," he said as he stood, lifting her with him, keeping their bodies joined.

"What the hell?" She gripped his shoulders, staring at him, her ankles locked behind his back.

"If I didn't know Arthur and Buddy were in the other room, I wouldn't give a crap about the goddamn banging, but holy hell, it's a buzzkill."

"Maybe this will help," she whispered in his ear as she raised her body up and then lowered it.

"Oh yeah." He sat down on the chair in front of the desk. "I like this position better anyway."

"Me too," she mused, rolling her hips and arching her back, giving him full access to her round breasts.

He suckled and pinched them while he flexed his feet, trying to maintain control. He focused on her body and how to please it, hoping he'd be able to give her another orgasm before he erupted.

Her moans bounced off the walls, tickling his ears like the wind sailing across the ocean. He gripped her hips, holding tight, gritting his teeth, but it wasn't going to stop the low, deep growl that vibrated from his throat.

"Duncan," she said in a breathy pant as she clamped down around him, her body shaking with release.

"Chastity," he whispered. "Beautiful Chastity." He kissed her neck as she dropped her head to his shoulder.

They held each other for a long moment, his hands running up and down her back, fingers drawing over her spine. He didn't want to let her go.

Knock! Knock!

"Duncan? Chastity?" Buddy called as the wood rattled.

"Open that door, and you're a dead man walking," Duncan yelled.

Chastity leaped from his lap, tripping over something, and her naked body hit the floor with a thud.

"Shit," she mumbled.

He quickly pulled her upright. "You okay?"

The door rattled.

"Hang on, asshole," Duncan yelled, holding her by the shoulders, staring into her wide eyes. "You better go get dressed before he comes in but try not to trip."

"Now who's the asshole?" She kissed his cheek, then turned and raced around the room for her clothes, tossing his at him.

He laughed, hiking up his pants. "Ready?"

"No but go ahead."

Duncan ran a hand through his hair, but it was hopeless. The entire room smelled of sex. He twisted the lock, then opened the door. "What is it?"

"We tried calling you both," Buddy said with his hands on his hips. "Something's going on down at the house. We need to move now."

16

Chastity hunched down behind Duncan in the woods on the east side of the house. Their entire plan had changed since a large van showed up. The team they had assembled flanked out around the perimeter but hid in the woods, not wanting to risk being seen. She adjusted her earpiece. Arthur had said no chatter unless necessary.

The silence was making her nuts.

"Look," Duncan said, pointing toward the back of the house where the van was parked. The door had been pushed open, and two men stood at attention with weapons.

"Over there," she said. "They took the guard from the front of the house."

Duncan tapped his ear. "Garth and Hawke, the front door is unmanned."

The sound of a rock hitting the roof echoed in the night. The man on top of the house turned toward the sound.

Chastity held her breath as Hawke raced across the yard. He pressed his back against the wall and peeked inside.

"Front room is clear," Hawke said. "Wait. I see movement."

"What is it?" Chastity asked, her heart racing so fast she figured everyone could hear it thump over the comms system.

"Girls. Not sure how many, but they are bringing them up from the basement."

"Fuck, they're moving them," Duncan said.

"Should we call that FBI agent?" she whispered. "Bo Ingalls."

"Text him." Duncan handed her his phone.

"Hawke, can you tell if the girls are handcuffed or restrained in any way?"

"I can," Arthur's voice crackled over the system. "And yes. They are. And one girl is wearing a plain blue dress."

"That's got to be Serenity," Chastity said,

excitement building in her stomach. She fumbled with Duncan's phone.

"Anyone have the Rossini boys in their sights? Or his uncle?" Duncan asked.

"The boys are here, but no sign of Anthony," Logan said. "He wasn't at his home either."

"He's here somewhere," Duncan mumbled.

"What should I tell Bo?" She held the phone in her trembling hands. Fighting fires came naturally, but a stakeout, not so much. Her cells burned her body and it felt like her entire body trembled with nervous energy. Her sister's safety was at stake and while she knew these men would do whatever it took, so many things could go wrong.

"Tell him we have intel on kidnapped girls and give him the location."

"Then what?" She stared at Duncan with horror-filled eyes. "We're not going to wait for them to come? You're not going to let them drive out of here?"

"That's exactly what we're going to do," Duncan said. "We've got a license plate, and we can follow."

"Keep the chatter down," Arthur commanded. "And Duncan is right."

"Like fucking hell," she mumbled, tossing the

phone at Duncan. It bounced off his shoulder and then hit the ground. She scanned the area, searching for a way to the van. If she slashed the tires, that would buy them some time.

The tree line of the woods circled the house, with a tiny clearing across the driveway. The man on the roof stood at the front, facing the water, but he would make his rounds soon enough. If she was going to do this, it had to be now.

"I'm not waiting," she said.

Duncan grabbed her by the arm. "Yeah, you are. And that's an order."

"I don't work for the Aegis Network and we're not fighting a fire. Listen, all I need to do is get to the van and slash a—"

"Chastity," Buddy interrupted. "I'm closer. I'll go."

"Wait," Ramey said. "That will be the first thing they see, and then they will know we're here. We can't risk that."

Out of the corner of Chastity's eyes, she saw a second man on the roof. He hadn't been there before. He pointed in her direction. "We've got a different problem," she said, taking out the binoculars. She focused on the second man when she felt cold metal against her temple and the click of a revolver. "Who do we have here?" a man's voice asked.

"Put the gun down," Duncan stood, but the man backhanded him with the butt of his weapon.

He groaned, falling to the ground like a dead fish.

The man grabbed her by the hair and yanked out her earpiece, tossing it to the ground and stepping on it. "Who are you?" the man demanded.

She recognized him as Anthony Rossini.

"Chastity Jade, and you've got my sister down there." She straightened her spine, determined to hold her ground. Her team would have heard Duncan before he was knocked out, and she knew they'd soon have a plan.

Only, she wouldn't be privy to it, which sucked.

"You're a little older than we normally deal in, but my clients always like a good sister fantasy."

She swallowed, hearing the sound of boots crunching against the tall grass. She held her breath, waiting to see someone from her team, but her lungs quickly deflated when the men turned out to be part of Rossini's gang. They lifted Duncan to his feet and started dragging him across the clearing. He groaned but was still unconscious.

"Move, honey." Rossini pressed his gun against her back.

Her team was watching. They had to be.

And they would move in soon enough. Until then, she had to make sure Duncan was okay.

———

When in danger, play dead.

It was a line from a book Duncan's mother read to him all the time when he and his siblings were little. It had stuck with him his entire life, but he never thought he'd ever use it until some asshole came and hit him with a gun in front of his girlfriend.

Okay, so it turned out to be Arthur's idea. Just as he was about to jump to his feet, Arthur's voice echoed in his brain to pretend to be knocked out.

Actually, Duncan wondered if maybe he'd been out for a second and he just thought he heard Arthur's voice since the earpiece had either fallen out or been removed.

Either way, it was too late to back out of his plan now.

He peeked his eyes open and glanced around as two men dragged him toward the house. He couldn't see Chastity, but he could smell her lilac perfume, so she had to be close.

"Let me look at my friend. He's bleeding pretty badly," Chastity said from somewhere behind him. Thank God.

He hadn't noticed the warm, tacky sensation until she mentioned blood. He'd been hit harder than that, but he was sure he was fine, other than the pounding headache and the fact that a fucking bastard held Chastity at gunpoint.

"Tell me who else is out there, and I'll think about it," Rossini said.

"Just me and him."

"And me," Buddy said. His voice came from the west, so maybe near the house.

The men dropped Duncan, and he groaned as he hit the ground face-first, right near the van. He hadn't realized he was that close, but that should be a good thing.

"Just the three of you?"

"Yes," Chastity said with a steady voice.

God, she was amazing. Cool under pressure. And she was his girlfriend.

"Well, either way, you're all dead," Rossini said. "Here, tie up your boyfriend."

Duncan opened one eye, and Buddy graced his

vision. He sat in a chair on the back porch, arms tied behind his back, and he had the audacity to wink.

Well, at least one man knew Duncan wasn't unconscious.

He moaned when Chastity took his arms and twisted them behind his back. When her hand reached inside his pocket, his body went rigid.

She placed the knife in his hand and pulled the cable cuff tight around his wrist. Well, not too tight.

Yep. Smart woman.

"Can I at least sit up?" he said, making his voice tremble.

"Sure thing." One of the men with guns hoisted him to his feet and shoved him on the porch, ramming his ass into a chair next to Buddy. The knife dug into his palm, and he groaned. Warm liquid trickled down his fingers.

He blinked, watching in horror as two men hoisted young girls, tied up, into the back of the van. He sucked in a breath when he eyed Serenity being shoved into the vehicle.

"Chastity!" Serenity tried to break free from the men pushing her, but they kept her restrained.

Chastity, on the other hand, charged forward,

but Rossini stepped in her way, hitting her stomach with the butt of a rifle.

"You fucking bastard. Touch my girlfriend again and I won't kill you quickly. I'll make you die a slow, miserable death." Duncan stood and took a fist to his jaw. He tumbled backward, landing on his side. The same guy who hit him yanked him to his feet, shoving him back into the seat.

"Right," Rossini said. "Let's go, boys. Get these girls out of here. We're running late." He lifted Chastity, cuffed her hands, and tossed her into the van. He closed the doors and banged on the metal.

"You're not going to get away with this," Duncan said behind a clenched jaw.

"I just did." Rossini smiled.

Brake lights filled the night sky as the van punched forward, kicking up gravel.

Buddy leaned over and whispered, "Just so you don't go all Rambo, Arthur is in the driver's seat."

That was pleasant news.

The van disappeared down the long driveway.

Duncan continued to fiddle with the knife, sawing at the plastic tie that bound his hands.

"Come on, boys, let's go," Rossini shouted again.

The only people still milling about were the two men who had dragged him across the yard.

"The boys are a little tied up," Ramey said as he stepped from the back of the house. Hawke and Garth followed, all three holding weapons. They pointed them at the bad guys, who raised their hands, including Joey.

"I wouldn't do that if I were you," Logan said as he walked from the woods behind the house. Dylan next to him.

Rossini turned just as Duncan freed his hands. "Oh, are you going to regret hitting my girl." Duncan lunged forward and swung right at Rossini's nose, hitting it square. Blood gushed as the man fell back. Duncan shook out his hand, a little surprised by the hardness of Rossini's face. He took a step forward, cocking his fist, but Buddy stopped him.

"He's not worth it," Buddy said, squeezing his biceps.

Duncan broke free and made his way to where Garrett had cuffed Joey. Duncan wanted to nail the little bastard, but instead, he poked him in the chest. "If you touched a single hair on Serenity's head, I will hunt you down, and I will kill you."

"Duncan. I think you should go to Chastity's side," Buddy said.

Flashes of lights filled the night sky. Three police cars and an unmarked vehicle sped down the driveway.

Duncan let out a long breath. "Where did Arthur take the girls?"

"To the inn," Buddy said, tossing him a set of keys. "We'll finish up here. Go."

"Thanks, man. For everything."

"Just don't tell my wife I let myself get tied up. It might give her some ideas. Pregnancy hormones have given her sex on the brain. Oh, and I told management about the headboard. Should be fixed by morning."

"You're an asshole."

"That's why I'm still your work wife."

"Everyone all right back there?"

Chastity let out a guttural sob when she heard Arthur's voice. "Get me out of these damn restraints."

"Yes, ma'am," Arthur said as the van stopped.

Seconds later, he pulled open the back doors. He cut through her restraints, then handed her a knife. "Take care of your sister."

"Thank you," she whispered as she gently took her sister's hands and helped release her from the cuffs. Sirens blasted in the distance. "I've got you," she whispered, holding her sister tight and stroking her hair.

Serenity clutched her around the waist, shivering and crying uncontrollably. Chastity kissed her forehead, rocking back and forth, trying to comfort her while she watched as Arthur carefully took care of the other girls, helping them into the ambulances that rolled in, along with a fire truck and a couple of state trooper vehicles. Minutes ticked by, and still no sign of Duncan.

She was sure his hands were full wrangling with all the bad guys.

Arthur made his way back to the van. "Let's get you and your sister in that ambulance." He pointed across the parking lot.

She nodded as Arthur wrapped his arms around her and her sister, helping them walk twenty paces. She sat on the back, still hugging her sister, whose sobs had turned into sniffles.

"Duncan will be here in a few minutes. I'll have the ambulance wait. Buddy said he should go to the hospital too."

"Thanks, Arthur. I owe you." Chastity nodded.

Arthur squeezed her shoulder. "Anything for one of my crew." He draped a blanket over their shoulders.

Serenity's shoulders bounced up and down with each heaving breath she took.

"It's going to be okay," Chastity said. "You're safe now."

"How did you find me?" Serenity asked between guttural sobs.

"Your journal helped. I knew that you hadn't run off. The rest, well, you can thank Duncan and the rest of my crew and their friends with the Aegis Network."

Serenity lifted her head. "You're pulling my leg."

"Nope." She cupped her sister's face. "Those are good men, and they put their lives on the line for you and all these girls."

"I screwed up so badly. Mom and Dad are going to kill me." Serenity dropped her head in shame.

"You did mess up, but the only thing Mom and Dad will do is hug you to death. Then maybe ground you until graduation."

"That's an entire year away," Serenity mumbled. "But you know what, after that ordeal, I don't think I like the real world too much right now."

"That's not daily life out here, so don't let that stop you from discovering exactly who you are. Dad mentioned you want to be a lawyer, and I think if you buckle down and do well in your senior year, they will let you live on campus."

Serenity wiped her face and laughed. "I thought about a defense attorney, but I think I'd rather be a prosecutor now."

"Good choice," Chastity said.

A car screeched to a halt, and Duncan raced from the driver's side.

"Hey, you," she said, unable to contain her smile. "Serenity, meet Duncan."

"As in, the guy, you're madly in love with?" Serenity asked.

Chastity saw no reason to hide her feelings anymore. If he didn't love her back, then so be it. "Yeah, that's the guy."

Duncan paused mid-step, his mouth gaping

open. "Did I hear that correctly? Did you say you love me?"

Chastity let out a long sigh. "No. My sister said that. But since we're on the subject, it might be true."

"Thank God, because I love you so much more." He stood in front of her with a wide smile. "And you..." He reached out and rested his hand on Serenity's shoulder. "If that asshole even so much as touched you, I want to know, so I can go back down that dirt road and beat the crap out of him."

Serenity let out a nervous laugh. "Thank you for saving us," she said as she jumped from the back of the ambulance and hugged Duncan.

"You're welcome," he said softly, holding her like a brother might. "Come on, let's get you both in this ambulance."

Chastity reached out and touched the side of Duncan's head.

He winced.

"I think you're going to need stitches," Chastity said.

"I feel like I have a worse hangover than after Buddy's birthday party last year." He made a face like he just swallowed a lemon.

"Oh God." She held her stomach as it pitched and swirled like she'd been on a roller coaster for weeks.

"You okay?"

She shook her head before racing off to the side of the ambulance. Thankfully, no one was around to see her lose her cookies, well, except Duncan, who once again held her hair back.

"What's wrong?" Serenity cried.

"Nothing," Chastity mumbled, wiping her mouth.

"But you just got sick," Serenity said.

"It happens when you're pregnant," Chastity admitted. No reason she couldn't tell her family. They should know first.

"What!" Serenity squealed. "You're going to have a baby? With him?"

"Nice," Arthur said as he rounded the corner and slapped Duncan on the back. "Congrats, dude. Now let's get all of you to the hospital. Chastity took a hard hit to the gut, and since she's with kiddo, we need to get that checked out."

"Wait, what? Chastity's going to have a kid with Duncan?" Buddy bent over, hands on knees, and busted out laughing. "Holy shit. Miracles do happen."

"Shut up, asshole," Duncan muttered.

Chastity's cheeks heated. When she'd made the admission, she hadn't meant to do it to anyone on the team yet—just family.

What was she thinking? They were family.

17

THREE WEEKS LATER...

Duncan stepped out onto the porch and stared at the wide-open spaces.

"Have a seat, son," George said from the rocking chair. His shotgun leaned against the railing.

Glancing at the two beers in his hands, Duncan couldn't decide whether to turn and run or drink both. He handed George one and eased into the other chair. "Beautiful night."

"It is indeed." George sipped before setting the drink on the small table and snagging his weapon, letting it rest across his lap. "I do appreciate all that you've done for my family. Risking your life to bring back my little girl means a lot."

"I was happy to do it, and honestly, it's what the Aegis Network is trained to do."

"You're a humble and honorable man." George shifted his gaze.

Duncan swallowed. Hard.

"And even a man of God, which is why I'm a little baffled that my daughter doesn't have an engagement ring on her finger." George lowered his chin.

"Actually, sir. That's what I wanted to talk to you about."

"Is it now." He ran his hand over the hard metal of his shotgun. "My wife and Chastity think they have kept me in the dark, but lets you and I be honest with one another, shall we?"

"Of course, sir. That's what I'm trying to do." He pounded his chest, clearing his throat. "I love Chastity and I'd like for your blessing."

"Are you asking for her hand in marriage?"

"Yes, sir, I am," Duncan said, reaching into his pocket. "This is my grandmother's ring and I'd like to ask Chastity tonight."

George cocked a brow. "And does my daughter know this will be happening?"

Jesus. This man wasn't going to cut him any slack. "Um, well, yes. We've discussed it."

"You know, back in my day, marriage came before the children. Before pregnancy. Before…" He smiled. "Oh, for the love all things holy. I can't keep this up." He set his gun to the side. "This was all Chastity's idea. She told me you were utterly terrified of me, which, if you were younger and didn't know what you wanted out of life, I might have been worried. But you love each other. You're good for each other. And I'm going to be a grandpa. What more could a man want." He stood, yanking Duncan from his chair. "Welcome to the family."

"You're not going to shoot me?"

"If you break my little girl's heart, I might." George slapped him on the back.

The front door screeched open and Chastity stepped outside with a bright smile. "Daddy, you're an old softie." She gave him a big hug and kiss on the cheek. "Now go away so I can get my ring."

Duncan laughed. "And you accuse me of taking all the romance out of everything." He slipped the ring onto her finger. "I love you. Will you do me the honor of being my wife?"

"Damn straight, it will be your honor." She raised up on tiptoe and kissed his cheek. "My mom made a big cake and she's already crying."

"Wait until we go back to my parents' house. It will be more of the same."

"I'm sure glad you carried me home that night," she said. "I'm going to enjoy loving you and watching you be a great father."

EPILOGUE

SEVEN MONTHS LATER...

Duncan stood over the bassinet, staring at his little girl, all swaddled up in a pink bunny blanket. He twisted his wedding ring, wondering how he'd gotten so lucky. He glanced over his shoulder. Chastity lay blissfully asleep in the hospital bed after eighteen hours of grueling labor. He wasn't sure who suffered more, his wife, or him having to watch the woman he loved more than anything go through such agonizing pain.

Only seconds after their daughter had been born, Chastity said it was worth it and she'd do it again.

He certainly wanted more, but he could be a patient man, even if he wasn't getting any younger.

The baby sighed. He reached in and rested his palm on her pudgy stomach. Poor thing was exhausted too.

"Hey, you," Chastity's sweet voice filled his ears. "She sleeping?"

He nodded. "You should be, too."

She stretched. "I've been sleeping for two hours. I'm sure she'll be up screaming to be fed." Chastity adjusted herself, and little baby girl Booker cried out as if on cue. "Bring her to me."

Duncan reached in and lifted her into his arms. He kissed her head and inhaled that fresh baby scent. "I can't believe how much I love this precious little thing. But we really need to find a name for her."

"I know," Chastity said.

Chastity's natural mothering ability amazed him. It wasn't much different than watching her at work. She did both as if that was what she was born to do. He, on the other hand, felt like a blubbering idiot when it came to taking care of his daughter.

He kissed the baby one more time before handing her to Chastity. The baby immediately turned her head and started looking for something to suck.

"I have never in my life seen a kid take to

breastfeeding like this one," Chastity said. "She's not even a day old yet."

"If she were a boy, I'd say something so inappropriate right now." He sat on the edge of the bed, humbled by his wife.

His wife.

It had only been a month since they got married. They hadn't wanted to rush, but the closer they got to the baby being born, the more he felt the need to make her his bride. Thankfully, she'd said yes and didn't mind a quick wedding at a local church with both their parents in attendance. It was a small wedding and they had yet to go on a honeymoon, but he didn't care. He had his family, and that's all that mattered now.

"So, what does she look like to you?" he asked. They'd tossed out a dozen or so girl names, but nothing felt right.

"If she were a boy, we would have named her after both our dads, so why not name her after both our moms?" Chastity asked.

"Laurie Ann," he whispered.

"Yeah. That sounds nice, don't you think?" Chastity glanced up at him, her ocean eyes tinged with happy tears.

He couldn't love anyone as much as he loved

her. She was the sun and the moon and everything in between.

"I like it," he said. "Laurie Ann Booker. It's a good name. An honorable one." He bent over, kissing first his wife, then his daughter. "I love both my girls."

"We love you more," Chastity said.

Thank you so much for reading DUNCAN'S HONOR. Please feel free to leave an honest review.

Next up in the series is GARTH'S HONOR.

If you haven't read the other Aegis Network Series, please check out the following:

THE AEGIS NETWORK
The Sarich Brother
The Lighthouse
Her Last Hope
The Last Flight
The Return Home
The Matriarch

Also, if you're curious about Darius Ford, check out his story here: **Darius' Promise**

Grab a glass of vino, kick back, relax, and let the romance roll in…

Sign up for my Newsletter (https://dl.bookfunnel.com/ 82gm8b9k4y) where I often give away free books before publication.

Join my private Facebook group (https://www.facebook. com/groups/191706547909047/) where I post exclusive excerpts and discuss all things murder and love!

ABOUT THE AUTHOR

Jen Talty is the *USA Today* Bestselling Author of Contemporary Romance, Romantic Suspense, and Paranormal Romance. In the fall of 2020, her short story was selected and featured in a 1001 Dark Nights Anthology.

Regardless of the genre, her goal is to take you on a ride that will leave you floating under the sun with warmth in your heart. She writes stories about broken heroes and heroines who aren't necessarily looking for romance, but in the end, they find the kind of love books are written about :).

She first started writing while carting her kids to one hockey rink after the other, averaging 170 games per year between 3 kids in 2 countries and 5 states. Her first book, IN TWO WEEKS was originally published in 2007. In 2010 she helped form a publishing company (Cool Gus Publishing) with *NY*

Times Bestselling Author Bob Mayer where she ran the technical side of the business through 2016.

Jen is currently enjoying the next phase of her life…the empty nester! She and her husband reside in Jupiter, Florida.

Grab a glass of vino, kick back, relax, and let the romance roll in…

Sign up for my Newsletter (https://dl.bookfunnel.com/82gm8b9k4y) where I often give away free books before publication.

Join my private Facebook group (https://www.facebook.com/groups/191706547909047/) where I post exclusive excerpts and discuss all things murder and love!

Never miss a new release. Follow me on Amazon:amazon.com/author/jentalty

And on Bookbub: bookbub.com/authors/jentalty

ALSO BY JEN TALTY

Brand new series: SAFE HARBOR!

Mine To Keep

Mine To Save

Mine To Protect

Mine to Hold

Mine to Love

Check out LOVE IN THE ADIRONDACKS!

Shattered Dreams

An Inconvenient Flame

The Wedding Driver

Clear Blue Sky

Blue Moon

Before the Storm

NY STATE TROOPER SERIES (also set in the Adirondacks!)

In Two Weeks

Dark Water

Deadly Secrets

Murder in Paradise Bay

To Protect His own

Deadly Seduction

When A Stranger Calls

His Deadly Past

The Corkscrew Killer

First Responders: A spin-off from the NY State Troopers series

Playing With Fire

Private Conversation

The Right Groom

After The Fire

Caught In The Flames

Chasing The Fire

Legacy Series

Dark Legacy

Legacy of Lies

Secret Legacy

Emerald City

Investigate Away

Sail Away

Georgia Moon

Jack Daniels

Jim Beam

Whiskey Sour

Whiskey Cobbler

Whiskey Smash

Irish Whiskey

The Monroes

Color Me Yours

Color Me Smart

Color Me Free

Color Me Lucky

Color Me Ice

Color Me Home

Search and Rescue

Protecting Ainsley

Protecting Clover

Protecting Olympia

Protecting Freedom

Protecting Princess

Protecting Marlowe

Rough Edge

Rough Beauty

The Brotherhood Protectors

The Saving Series

Saving Love

Saving Magnolia

Saving Leather

Hot Hunks

Cove's Blind Date Blows Up

My Everyday Hero – Ledger

Tempting Tavor

Malachi's Mystic Assignment

Needing Neor

Holiday Romances

A Christmas Getaway

Alaskan Christmas

Whispers

Christmas In The Sand

Heroes & Heroines on the Field

Taking A Risk